Quong awoke suddenly from a deep sleep. He had stayed up late the night before, celebrating with his sister. This was the season of the lunar year — Tet 1968. The pounding in his head was from more than the vast quantity of ba si da he had drunk. The potent rice wine was known for its delayed action but not like what he was feeling now.

Before he could regain his senses, his head and body were rocked by a violent explosion. For a fleeting moment he thought perhaps it was a large number of fireworks. The dust falling from the ceiling dispelled this theory. Quong knew this was no friendly Tet celebration.

The third explosion threw him onto the floor of the small two-room house in which he had lived for the last two years.

Things were never the same for Quong or Vietnam after Tet 1968.

OPERATION BRIGHTEYES

PAUL SINOR

LYNX BOOKS
New York

OPERATION BRIGHTEYES

ISBN: 1-55802-229-5

First Printing published 1987
Lynx Edition/September 1988

Published by special arrangement with Daring Books

This is a work of fiction. Names, characters, places, and incidents are either the product of the author's imagination or are used fictitiously. Any resemblance to actual events, locales, or persons, living or dead, is entirely coincidental.

This book is published by Lynx Books, a division of Lynx Communications, Inc., 41 Madison Avenue, New York, New York, 10010. The name "Lynx" together with the logotype consisting of a stylized head of a lynx is a trademark of Lynx Communications, Inc.

Printed in the United States of America

0 9 8 7 6 5 4 3 2 1

To the lady in my life.
Without you this would not be.

OPERATION BRIGHTEYES

ABOUT THE AUTHOR

PAUL SINOR is a U.S. Army Lieutenant Colonel currently assigned to the National Committee for Employer Support of the National Guard and Reserves, a department of the Defense Agency. He is a Vietnam veteran and has worked extensively with the Vietnamese "boat people." He writes with a first-hand understanding of the land and people involved in **Operation Brighteyes,** both United States and the Vietnamese. He has had numerous articles published in various military and civilian magazines.

OPERATION BRIGHTEYES

CHAPTER 1

Eddie Wilson watched the rain as it fell on the ground outside his room. He watched it every day during the rainy seasons. Each day it was the same. The rain, like Eddie, was taken for granted: both were expected to be there; both always were.

The heavy downpour saturated the area, creating a watersoaked landscape as far as his eyes could see. The dirt and gravel road along which the water flowed was marked with pock holes. Each hole was filled with water. The run-off moved swiftly in ditches along the sides of the main road and its one artery leading up to the old building. From inside the building it all looked the same . . . water everywhere.

The rain continued to fall and would probably do so for several more weeks. The dark clouds overhead gave no indication of a break in the weather. The water created innumerable small streams that rushed and swirled mindlessly in every direction. The streams carried bits of twigs, trash, and other seemingly insignificant articles with them.

The rain falls for over two months during this period. This was the beginning of the summer monsoon season in which virtually everything in Southeast Asia becomes a part of the rain. Water fell as if a giant container had been hoisted skyward then tipped over, spilling the contents so rapidly it was impossible to identify individual drops. Once on the ground, the water took on a dirty brown hue. It stood in the well-defined squares of land, which would soon turn green as the rice planted in them began to grow and mature. Only the ditches, the dikes, and an occasional canal kept the ground water moving. Where there were no canals or ditches, the water found its own method of claiming the land and people. It simply flooded. Everything and everyone became a part of it. Nothing escaped, neither land nor people.

The man watched silently as the rain fell. It covered the earth he claimed as his own. Long ago he had mentally laid claim to all he could see to the left and right of the barred door covering his cell.

He had been part of the monsoons for seven years . . or was it eight? The first two years were now almos a blur in his memory. The time was like a bad phonograp record; he could replay it, but it was distorted, scratchec warped.

Wilson, Edward B., Captain, US Army, 05344471, peered between the bars on the door of his cell in An Bac Province, Republic of South Vietnam. His world consisted of only what he could see when he looked through these bars. He had been here since his move from Viet Cong control to being the responsibility of the North Vietnamese Regulars running the POW and re-education camp in An Bac.

Since his capture in the U Minh Forest in 1971, he had been shuttled between camps on a regular basis. Most of the moves occurred during the first two years. All took him to yet another jungle camp. These small stark camps were operated by local force Viet Cong. During those first two years, spent deep in the southwest portion of the Mekong Delta, he saw only one other Caucasian prisoner.

He was an Australian Warrant Officer named Jefferies. When Eddie saw him, the Aussie looked like a star in one of the films the Army did about the liberation of Auschwitz or Dachau. Jefferies was so frail his hip bones were protruding from his body, to the point where they were breaking through his almost paper-thin skin. Although they suffered together for two months at one camp, Wilson spoke to him only once, during a stop when their guards bought rice and pineapples for themselves. When Eddie was finally moved to a location by himself, Jefferies was at the point of crawling, for he was far too weak to walk. Why the VC kept him was a mystery Eddie never solved.

Considering the wretched condition the officer had been in when they spent their last three days together, in a small hamlet at the southern edge of the forest, it would have been a miracle if the Australian lived another six months. That was six years ago. Jefferies was surely dead by now.

Eddie Wilson was not. He was alive. More so some days than others, but he was very much alive. How and why was something he asked himself constantly. The fact remained that Eddie Wilson was alive and was still being held captive in An Bac Province, Republic of South Vietnam. The mystery was not that he was alive but that he was still there, still being held by the Viet Cong.

Captain Eddie Wilson surprised even himself when he allowed his mind to regress over the years since his capture. It was not good to let the mind roam uncontrolled and Eddie knew it. It could, and often did, play vicious tricks. The mind must stay active. It must be fed doses of challenges, even trivial questions like baseball batting averages. Who won the pennant in '46? Who was the Sunday School teacher that summer spent with Aunt Bonnie in Florida? Because his life and sanity depended on it, these were questions begging for answers.

Why was he still alive? He had taken his quota of beatings and torture. He had not been a model prisoner. Eddie had one unsuccessful escape attempt to his credit. He had a thousand whys he could not answer. All he could do was ask. Because he asked, he had to provide both the questions and the answers.

Eddie watched the rains as the summer monsoon's flood of trash-laden water swirled through the camp. He saw the water move along the ground next to the brick stucco wall. Occasionally it flooded and seemed to stall momentarily as it filled one of the large indentations made by rocket and grenade fragments during the last days of the war in An Bac. Just as the exploding ordnance had left its mark on the wall, the water left a dirty brown stain on everything it touched.

Eddie watched the swiftly moving stream with eager anticipation this morning. Bobbing in the flow, less than fifty feet from him, was an orange. A piece of fresh fruit! Extra food would shortly be within his grasp. With luck and patience, the prize would soon be his.

The small orange bobbed and dipped, and occasionally completely disappeared under water, as it closed the distance to him.

"Easy now, Wilson," he said, as the fruit spun into a large indentation in the old wall. "It'll come out. Just be patient, son. Just be patient." No longer did it seem strange for him to be talking aloud to himself; after all, he had no one else to talk to. He softly encouraged himself as he watched the fruit. When he was a child, his grandmother had explained that it was acceptable to talk to yourself if you didn't get into a two-way conversation. Insanity was a certain fate for anyone who asked himself a question and then provided the answer, she said. If this was true, Eddie had already crossed the thin line protecting the insane from those professing sanity.

He now had an almost unobstructed view of the orange through the bars in his cell door. Once it was close enough, he could quickly grab it. He could reach for it between the bars. When he was first captured his arms would have been too muscular to fit between the metal bars, but in his present condition this posed no problem.

Like a cobra attacking its prey, Eddie's arm exploded through the water, grabbing the orange when it finally came into range. He was on his knees with his body pressed tight against the metal-barred door to his cell. Wilson knelt in the water for almost a minute without moving, his arm still extended with the orange in his hand. No guard had seen or heard him.

He retreated from the door and stood up. Like a small child at Christmas, he slowly, and with great interest, examined the prize he now held in his hand.

It was a small yellowish-brown piece of fruit native to the surrounding area. The baseball-size orange had probably been dropped by a guard. It almost certainly came from the local market place.

Once he had it in his possession, he took the time to admire his prize. Eddie held the fruit up to eye level and slowly turned it in his hand as he visually feasted on it.

The face staring at the orange was a gaunt, thin face. It had a beard and a mustache, sunken eyes, and a greatly receding hair line. There were a few yellow teeth left in his mouth. Most of the others had been knocked out during the first two years. One had been pulled slowly, and with great delight, by a guard wielding a pair of pliers, during the torture session after his escape attempt. Even with the losses, there were still enough teeth left to eat the meager daily ration of rice and soup with an occasional piece of meat or fish.

He wore sandals made from old tires. The first time he had seen a pair of these a friend was sending them home as a war trophy. They were called Ho Chi Minh racing slicks. The thick black rubber soles were secured to his feet with small pieces of rope. The water now covered his feet as high as his ankles. His ragged blue pants covered thin hairy legs. The torn pants came only to mid-thigh.

His once muscular body was now a fading memory compared to his now lean frame. Only his tan remained. Years prior to his trip to sunny southeast Asia, he had spent hours playing tennis or simply stretched out on the beach or pool-side to develop his tan. He was now tanned to a dark, almost mahogany, color from exposure to the blazing sun which greeted his work detail or his movement outside his cell. The tan, he thought, made a nice contrast to the color of the delectable piece of fruit he was now preparing to feast upon. Like an animal dragging a fresh kill to its den, Eddie slowly moved to the far corner of the cell which had become both his dungeon and his castle.

The tiny cell contained all his worldly possessions. He had been allowed to keep a wooden box in which he placed his rice bowl, a spoon, an enameled cup, a candle, a pencil and a small ball of twine he had managed to accumulate while on work details. The box still had traces of the markings from its former contents: GRENADES M2LOT 2275019 RIA. At one time he had had another pair of faded blue pants. He had kept them rolled up in a corner of the box, but he had been forced to start wearing them when his old ones finally rotted away. The pants and sandals were his only clothing. For work details his guards occasionally gave him a shirt which was taken back at day's end.

The most important and valuable item in his room was the tattered mosquito net covering the rack upon which he slept. Without it, sleep was impossible. The mosquitoes in the Mekong Delta were a vicious lot and bit without regard to nationality or status. Guard and prisoner alike were fair game for the tiny airborne bloodsuckers.

The net covered a rack made of long thin round limbs, worn smooth by hours spent upon them. The Viets used their racks for bed, table, chair or anything else requiring a strong flat surface. It had been so long since Eddie had felt the soft firmness of a mattress, he couldn't imagine sleeping on anything other than the rack upon which he now sat.

Force of habit taught him not to take anything for granted; therefore, he slowly surveyed his surroundings prior to beginning his feast.

Three sides of his cell were enclosed in a white brick covered with well-marked stucco. The only light came from the end of his cell, secured by a door with iron bars. Looking at the rusty metal, Eddie felt certain he could have bent them, or at least pulled them out of place enough to allow escape, during the first few months of his imprisonment. In his condition, that was out of the question now.

He wasn't sure of exact dimensions but he had measured his cell with every imaginable method since his capture. It was exactly seventeen of his feet long and seven-and-one-half feet wide. This equated to thirty-seven hand lengths or two hundred twenty-one fingers long. The combinations were endless. There were one hundred seventy-two little bumps or knots where branches had been removed from the limbs making up his rack. There were sixty-six nails and twelve screws in the box holding his possessions. Sometimes he thought himself crazy for counting, and at other times he knew this was a major part of his effort to keep from losing his sanity.

He often played trivia with himself. He worked mentally for days trying to remember answers to questions he asked himself. Many times he knew he didn't know the answer to a question but he asked it anyway. Sometimes he simply made up an answer. What difference did it make? After all, other than Eddie, who the hell cared? Eddie did. He had to.

Experience had taught Eddie two things about food. Eat it immediately and waste nothing. With this in mind, he slowly peeled his orange and placed the thin pieces of peeling in his rice bowl for future use.

It was not often that he got anything other than the cabbage and vegetable soup fed him twice daily with a small bowl of rice. When he was with his first captors in the U Minh, at least he occasionally got coconuts or bread fruit. His favorite fruits, though, were the little bo dao or rose apples as the Americans called them. These crisp juicy yellow fruits had a sweet taste and the distinctive flavor and smell of fresh roses. Prior to his capture, Eddie and his Vietnamese counterpart often bought them on the local market.

Eddie occasionally wondered about his old Vietnamese counterpart, Dai Uy Hua. At the time of their first meeting, they were both first lieutenants. The Vietnamese and his American ally were promoted to Dai Uy, or captain, within a month of each other.

They were on a search and destroy mission in the U Minh when the company of Regional Forces were drawn into an ambush by a company of hard-core Viet Cong with North Viet Regular cadre. It was almost over before any of the three American advisors could get on a radio and call for gunships or artillery support.

A grenade explosion between Eddie and Hua was, ironically, the incident that both saved his life and led to his capture. He re-lived the firefight in daylight and in darkness. Neither time nor sleep could blot out those final few seconds when he saw the crude hand grenade hit the ground. Before Eddie could react, Hua yelled, "Dai Uy Wilson," and covered the grenade blast with his own body.

The explosion had sufficient force to knock Eddie unconscious momentarily. The only merciful result was that the blast killed Hua instantly. When Eddie regained his senses, the first thing he noticed was his weapon was missing. For the second time in less than two minutes, a cruel twist of fate had him in its grasp.

Local policy dictated by the Viet Cong was very explicit on the capture of American advisors. Medics could be taken prisoner unless they were armed. Sergeants who had weapons could be taken captive unless the weapons had been recently fired. All medics with weapons and sergeants with recently fired weapons were to be shot. All officers, their counterparts and interpreters were to be shot immediately.

For the first six months of his imprisonment, Eddie Wilson agonized over the fact that he alone of his advisory team survived. Since none of the men wore rank or carried ID's, the Viet Cong didn't know he was an officer. Why did he survive? How did they select him to live? Certainly he had no death wish, but why was he spared?

There would be no work detail today. The rains had once again put an end to the meager amount of physical labor Eddie was able to accomplish.

These days of no work were met with mixed emotion. Although the labor was taxing, it was not unbearable. At least it got him out of his cell. When he was not on work detail, occasionally the guards would take him into the the commandant office for "debriefings." It was obvious to all that he had no current military information to give them so it usually turned into a session where they simply screwed around with him.

After so many years with the Viets, Eddie spoke the language with ease. Now when the Commandant spoke to him, he spoke in Vietnamese and in most sessions spoke slowly enough for Eddie to follow. "We now have heard that your president has welcomed home all the men who refused to take arms against the people of Vietnam." The Major, whom Eddie nicknamed B.O. because of his apparent aversion to bathing, leaned closer across his desk as he spoke. "What do you think of this?"

With head bowed, his response should have been an agreement with the policy and delight that the President of the United States now recognized the men were correct in their refusal to wage war.

Perhaps it was his luck in getting the orange, maybe it was the rain, but an obvious outside force made Eddie react, not in the prescribed manner.

"I think it is good these men are home. I also think I should be with them. Send me to America and I will tell them what they missed by not coming to your country. I can---"

Before he could finish, the Commandant slapped him out of the chair in which he sat.

"You fool! Do you not believe I could have you killed? My word is enough. I could do it myself. Take him back. No food for two days!" The Commandant spat the words as Eddie lay on the floor.

This was not a normal session, and Eddie was unsure why he spoke as he did. All he had had to do was attend the session and listen to the usual lies and respond accordingly.

They usually told him obvious lies about what was happening in the world and the United States, to test his reaction. He had been told at various times that Vietnam had captured all of Asia to include Japan and India, the population of the state of California had all been killed by venereal disease and that the U.S. had been destroyed in a war between blacks and whites. The proper response to these statements was outrage and dismay. Once done, he was returned to his cell to reflect on what he had been told. To argue or disagree brought punishment.

Here in this compound he had managed to establish a somewhat uneasy friendship with one of the guards. Although he usually saw him only one day a week, the man would talk to Eddie in broken English. From their conversations Eddie suspected his guard had been a Chieu Hoi during the war. The Chieu Hois were Viet Cong or NVA who defected to the side of the South Viets and fought against their former comrades. As the war drew to an end, many saw the error of their judgment and went back quietly to a different V.C. unit in another part of the country.

Eddie gave each of his guards nicknames. This one he called "Jack." The guard didn't realize it, but he had been named for a dog Eddie had as a young boy. Since he was the only friendly companion Eddie now had, somehow it seemed appropriate.

Jack had a wife or girl friend who also worked at the compound. She was a cook in the large open kitchen used to feed all the personnel assigned to the compound.

It was during his third year in the compound that Eddie heard of other Americans in the area. At first it was by way of bits and pieces of conversation between guards. Once he actually saw two men, one black and one white, in a jeep as it passed by him. As soon as his guard saw him looking at the two men, he shoved Eddie face down into the drainage ditch in which he was working.

For over a year, he tried to piece together these bits of conversation and information. Why was he unable to see them? Why did he not have them on work detail with him? Who were they? How many were in the area? What shape, physically and mentally, were they in? Why had they not been released?

Jack supplied some of the missing pieces. Little by little as their fragile association grew, Eddie found out more about his location, his guards, his reason for being there and the Americans he had spotted.

"Why am I in the country of the North Vietnamese?" he asked Jack one day.

"It is all country of the North now. Even here in An Bac. There is no South Vietnam any more." Jack responded with nationalistic pride as he told Eddie the name of the Delta province in which they were located.

He was in An Bac Province and was in an old American Army compound. His original captors had not reported his existence to the local V.C. commander until after the return of those U.S. POWs acknowledged by the North Viets. To acknowledge his capture meant to account for him, something they were unwilling to do.

The most startling revelation was about the other Americans. Jack finally told him they were in separate houses in an adjoining compound. Jack had seen eight of them, all living in two-man rooms.

"If you will put all the Americans in this cell you can learn English quicker. You will have more men to talk to." Wilson baited Jack for information on the others.

"No. They are special. They sleep on the other side of the compound. You will not talk to them." Jack spoke so matter-of-factly that Eddie did not broach the subject again for several months.

Eddie was quite interested and concerned about who these others were. With the exception of the two he had seen in the jeep, he had seen no other Americans. There was a possibility that one of the men was his old Executive Officer, Mike Russell. He did not know for sure whether Mike had been killed or captured that day so long ago, but he could always hope that the wiry little guy from Arkansas had made it.

His only hope of finding out more about these Americans lay in getting Jack to tell him. This was something the guard had been unable or unwilling to do. All Eddie could do was speculate on who, how many and why.

It would do him no good to dwell on it. His objective was to make one more sunrise and sunset. One day at a time. He could do it that way. He could muster enough strength to make one day. He would worry about next week when it was one sunset away.

As far as Eddie was concerned, no one knew he was alive. No one knew and no one cared.

He was wrong.

CHAPTER 2

Phong V. Quong was on his way to the American Embassy when the last helicopter left Vietnam. It left without him and without hundreds, perhaps thousands, of Vietnamese nationals who believed in the survivability of the government of South Vietnam and in the promises of the Americans. Many Vietnamese were not as fortunate as Quong. They did not escape the advancing Communists. These men and women were systematically executed or "neutralized," as the North Vietnamese Army preferred to call it. Quong managed to melt into the advancing wave of refugees and became an unknown member of postwar Saigon.

Quong and his sister were trying to make their way through the multitudes of people on Cong Lea, past the massive American air base, Ton Son Nhut, when the end came. At the time they felt no hatred, but rather disappointment in the Americans they had both served. Quong worked at the MACV Headquarters, and his sister Bea worked in one of the hotels which had been taken over by the military just outside the main gate of Ton Son Nhut. Neither talked of the other's involvement with the war effort or the Americans.

Quong pulled his sister into the alley beside the

Maryland BOQ. It offered them a few minutes' shelter from the mass confusion of the streets.

"What do you wish to do now?" Quong spoke loud enough for Bea to hear him above the street noise. "We have few options left. One thing is certain, we must leave the city. It will not be safe for us in Saigon."

Bea looked at her only brother as they prepared to debate quickly a series of decisions which could provide them new lives or cause the young man and woman untold hardship, which would almost certainly include death for collaboration.

"I will do what you think is best for us." Fear was beginning to turn to terror on her face. "I have all I own with me now. There is no reason to return to my house. We must leave the city. But to where?"

Quong had come to Saigon in 1964, from a small village in the Mekong Delta where his family had lived for as long as anyone could remember. His people were rice farmers and did not understand the problems and politics involved in the war. They wanted only to be left alone and be allowed to plant and harvest rice, fish and go to market, as they and their ancestors had done since the days prior to the Japanese invasion and the French rout under Ho Chi Minh.

It was a chance meeting with a cousin that kindled the fire of curiosity in Quong. Nguyen was home on leave from the ARVN Army. "Nguyen, why have you returned to Ap Binh Tay? Is the war over? Do you come back to start a family?" Quong's ignorance of the war amused his cousin. "If you had seen the cities I have seen in the last year you would not ask if I will return. I've seen places you have never even heard of. Da Lat, Pleiku, Hue. These are cities in the mountains. I have heard, though I never saw it, that it snows in Da Lat!"

Once again, as Quong failed to register the expected

awe at these words, both he and Nguyen realized he had much to learn about life beyond his village.

He told of the jobs to be had and money to be made by a smart strong country boy. It took little persuasion to entice Quong to trade his native village for Saigon.

Quong's journey to Saigon took three days. It covered one hundred eighty miles. Quong began by taking a taxi boat from his local village market place to Can Tho, the largest city in the Delta.

Quong had heard many stories of the great market places and activities in Can Tho, but seeing it for the first time was almost too much for him. Never before had he seen so many people and so much activity. If asked to describe it to his family, he would have taken days to relate the sights and sounds. It was beyond description for him. If only Bea could see this, he thought, as he wandered through the central market place along the Mekong River. "Our crops would bring a great number of piasters here," he said to a street vendor. Unlike the people of the Ap Binh Tay market place, the seller simply ignored his comment.

His father had given him the little cash money the family had. It was the equivalent of three U.S. dollars, but with it he had to feed himself and make his way on to Saigon.

Many of the sights in Can Tho impressed him, but the thing which caught his attention was the largest U.S. Special Forces camp at Binh Tuoy. Here many of his fellow countrymen were employed in a variety of jobs. Nguyen gave him the name of a man to talk to at the base. It was the only contact his cousin had provided him in the world beyond Ap Binh Tay.

Quong waited outside the gate at Binh Tuoy, as he had no pass which would grant him access. He asked everyone going in that morning who would stop and talk to him if they knew the man whose name his cousin had given him. At last one responded favorably and said he would tell the man that Quong was waiting at the gate.

The Americans on base had adopted the Vietnamese custom of a two-hour midday break, and everyone used it to eat, sleep or conduct other business. Quong and his contact could talk at that time.

Outside the gate, Quong mingled with many vendors and pedicab drivers stationed across the road, within easy access of any American who wished to partake of their wares or services. Many times during the morning, he saw an American arrive with a Vietnamese girl friend.

Even in 1964, the American influence had begun to have an effect on the customs and dress of the women of Vietnam. Quong saw many of the women dressed in fashions new to him, western dress. They had begun to discard the traditional dress of Vietnam, the ao dai, in favor of slacks or dresses. The women wore coloring on their faces and lips. Ornate jewelry hung from around their necks and wrists, and they had the pleasant smell of western perfume.

Although he was not formally educated and could not even read or write, Quong got an important education that day as he waited. If he wanted to succeed within this new society taking over his country, he must learn the secrets of who and what could help him gain employment with the people on the other side of the road. That was the key. If he was to prosper in the new Vietnam he must move to the other side of the road.

At precisely twelve noon, the local Vietnamese began a systematic exodus from the Special Forces Compound. Some walked, but many rode their own bicycles, a mark of wealth in those early days of the war. As he waited, the man with whom he had talked earlier in the morning and another man came up to him. Both were on bicycles.

The new man was dressed in camouflaged fatigues and wore a beret of a similar pattern on his head. Quong was immediately impressed with this stranger standing before him. Perhaps his cousin was right. This man could help get him established in Saigon.

"Chao Ong," said Quong as he gave a courteous bow, being careful not to overdo it. The traditional greeting was returned by the uniformed stranger. He then asked what he could do for the cousin of his old friend, Nguyen.

"It has been a long time since I have seen your cousin. Is he well?" As he talked, he guided Quong and the other man about fifty meters from the gate to one of the many roadside stands catering to the food needs of the Vietnamese.

"There is nothing wrong with him, is there?" Mixed with a voice of certain authority was a note of concern. "Is it he you want to talk about, or is it you?"

"I am on my way to Saigon, and I do not know anyone who will help me find a job. I would like to work for the Americans." Quong tried not to sound too simple in this request. After all, Nguyen said there were thousands of the American military and civilians in their country, and they needed all the local help they could get.

The men moved to a roadside hut where the stranger purchased bowls of rice and fish for the three of them. "What can you do?" asked his new-found friend between mouthfuls of rice. "Can you speak English so you can be an interpreter? Can you guide the Americans to where the Viet Cong hide, as I do?" he said with obvious pride in his role as scout. "Are you willing to cook or sew for the men in Saigon? What services can you offer?"

This was something Quong had not thought about. He assumed he would simply go to Saigon, get a job and send for any other members of his family wanting to join him. Quong must think long and hard prior to answering this question, for a wrong answer might insult his contact and then he would not try to help him.

"I have been told that I have talent as an nghe si. Perhaps I could do that."

"I doubt there is a great need for artists in Saigon, but the Americans feel they must draw everything out prior to going on an operation. We have a very good nghe si in my office who draws only lines on boards. The Americans call them charts. Perhaps you could get a position in Saigon as an artist of lines." The three of them found this to be worth a laugh, and it was the first time Quong heard the stranger speak with anything less than the most serious of voices.

Quong's friend took a small green notebook from the right breast pocket of his camouflaged fatigues and began to write on it. Quong felt the note was about him, and for the first time in his life he wished he could read.

"Take this note and find Dai Uy Thomas. He is a captain with the U.S. Army in Saigon. You can find him in the Carolina Hotel. I have written that you are an excellent artist and a good friend of mine. Do not disappoint him or me, for I will not forget this. Someday you may be able to assist me when I come to Saigon. If I ever call on you, I will expect you to do so without question. You will need money in Saigon. Do you have enough?"

"I have a few piasters left. My family could not give me much when I left." Quong held out his hand to reveal less than six hundred P's remaining.

"That will not even buy a ticket to Saigon." Once again the man dug into the top pocket of the shirt and came out with more piasters than Quong had ever seen one person have. "I am going to loan you one thousand piasters. I expect to get it back. Do not try to send it; I will collect it in person when I see you in Saigon."

The note and small pile of one hundred piaster notes

were placed in Quong's hand, and the meeting came to an end almost instantly as the two men got up to leave.

It took almost two years for Quong to learn the identity of his mysterious benefactor. He had once been a Viet Cong Regimental Commander and had defected to the side of the GVN when word got out that the Americans were taking defectors and paying them to be scouts and operate in their old areas. The Americans called them Kit Carson Scouts; the Viet Cong called them dao ngu . . . turncoats! His friend, Ltc. Twee, had had a reward of over two thousand U.S. dollars put on his head by his former NVA associates.

Quong walked back to the main market place in Can Tho. He asked directions to where he could catch a bus for Saigon and was directed to the Bien Xa Moi district of Can Tho.

By 1964, Bien Xa Moi was taking on the appearance of a sin strip, catering to the every need of the U.S. military personnel in the Delta. There were tailor shops where custom-made suits could be obtained, from merchants who were themselves foreign to Vietnam. Several bars lined one alleyway, and there was a sign across the front of one building that was completely foreign to Quong. The big red letters spelled out MASSAGE PARLOR. Although he could not read, he could identify most types of business by the items displayed in the windows. There was no hint of the activities in this establishment, as those people entering immediately went behind a door just inside the main entrance. He did notice, however, that a brisk business was being conducted and it was all between U.S. men and Vietnamese women.

Quong spent his first night sleeping on the ground across from the bus stop. He could not take a chance on missing the bus to Saigon the next morning.

The bus from Can Tho made its final stop in Saigon

about one mile from the Carolina. Quong covered the distance on foot, stopping many times to ask directions. He traveled slowly on purpose. The sights and sounds of the city were as he had never imagined. Never had he seen so many shops selling such a variety of goods. These items were as foreign to him as the new city in which he walked.

Hanging in some shop windows were machines which made music. Quong had never seen or heard a radio. The only music he ever heard was the loud crashing of cymbals and bells and the wild frantic beating of drums during a Buddhist funeral, when evil spirits were scared away from the brightly colored boat or other conveyance carrying the remains to its gravesite.

Rings and jewelry of every type flashed in the sunlight as he passed. Food, meat and drink, strange to him, were offered by vendors, both inside and outside the shops. He wished he could spend more time getting better acquainted with the things and people he saw, but he must get to the Carolina and meet Dai Uy Thomas.

Quong stopped his walk long enough to purchase a loaf of banh mi. These were the small loaves of bread the French had taught the Vietnamese to bake. Along with the bread, he got a glass of nuoc chanh, a lemonade made with the small lemons native to the country. The food was the first he had eaten since his meeting the day before with the two men at the Binh Tuoy Special Forces Camp.

He didn't realize it had been over twenty-four hours since he had last eaten, until the pleasant shock to his taste buds reminded him.

The walk took almost an hour. By the time he reached the Carolina, the traditional two-hour lunch break had already started. Perhaps I will be lucky and find Dai Uy Thomas today, thought Quong, as he made his way to the front entrance of the hotel.

The Carolina Hotel had once been used by French dignitiaries while they visited Saigon, the Paris of the Orient. It had, at one time, been the home of the French Ambassador and a number of lesser French officials, during the colonial days prior to the first Vietnamese war of the early fifties. It still maintained the stately dignity of a great structure, but twenty years of use by civilians and military had taken its toll. The grand balcony overlooking the streets of Saigon now served as a meeting place for the U.S. military advisors and their counterparts in the ARVN. One could see that the upper crust of the population of Saigon still frequented the restaurant, oblivious to the men dressed in fatigues, many even carrying sidearms, who were interspaced with civilians there.

Quong was met at the entrance by a man in a white coat and black tie. "Where do you think you are going?" asked the man roughly of Quong as he barred the door. "You cannot come in here; we do not allow beggars."

"Beggar?" Quong cut him off in mid-sentence, "I have never begged for anything. I am looking for Dai Uy Thomas."

"Why are you looking for Dai Uy Thomas?" asked the man as he continued to block the door.

"I have a message for him. It's very important."

By now several of the people in the restaurant were aware of the commotion at the door and turned to see what was happening.

In Vietnam, one of the most valuable assets an American advisor could have was an interpreter. Without one, most of the men sent there could not function. At times an interpreter could be even more valuable than a weapon. In a firefight Viet troops would go out of their way to protect their advisor and his interpreter, as they were the lifeline to supplies, support, and to the abundance of the American Post Exchange system.

Vin Key Sua was the interpreter for Captain Thomas, and he was sitting in the restaurant of the Carolina waiting for the Captain when the argument between Quong and the headwaiter started.

He arose and spoke sharply to the headwaiter. "Let him in. I will see what he wants," he said, as he made his way to the door and took Quong by the arm. "Now, peasant, what do you want with Dai Uy Thomas? You said you had a note for him. Let me see it."

"I'm sorry, sir, but I cannot give it to anyone but the Dai Uy. It comes from a man at the Binh Tuoy Special Forces Camp." Quong felt that to give up the note was to give up his only means of securing a job in Saigon.

"You fool," said Vin, as he pushed Quong into the corner by the door. "Do you want to tell everyone in Saigon where we have placed Special Forces Camps? You are either very simple or stupid. Either way, I can't leave you here by yourself. Come to my table. Dai Uy Thomas will be here in a little while."

Quong would get to meet the Dai Uy, but he was not sure how hospitable he would be towards him.

Quong drank only tea as the two men waited in silence for Captain Thomas to arrive.

An American jeep stopped in front of the Carolina and the American sitting in the passenger's side of the vehicle stepped out. The Vietnamese driver continued on his way, leaving the American standing by the curb. The American climbed the six steps to the entrance in three lopes.

As he made his way to the table, Vin rose to meet him, and motioned for Quong to do the same.

"Chao Ong," said Vin.

"Another cousin from Da Nang?" said Captain

Thomas as he sat down and motioned the waiter to return to the table.

"Not this time, Dai Uy. I have never seen this man before, but he came in here looking for you. He said he had a message for you from someone at the S.F. camp in Binh Tuoy. I stopped him before he could give any more information to the headwaiter."

The conversation between Vin and the Captain was in English, so the only words Quong could understand was the reference to Binh Tuoy. The pitch of Vin's voice told of his displeasure with Quong.

"I don't think he's given away any great military secrets, Vin. The camp at Binh Tuoy is so large now that anybody within ten miles of it can simply follow the pedicabs coming and going and they have a fix on the place."

"Let's see the note, slick," said Captain Thomas as he extended his hand.

"Well, well, Vin. It's from Truong Ta Twee, the old Lieutenant Colonel we sent to Binh Tuoy after he came across up in Xeon last year. He recommends Quong to us for use as a chart maker in MACV Headquarters." He turned to Quong, "Have you ever worked for the GVN or Americans before?" Quong could only stare back at him.

"Just once I'd like to have someone come looking for a job who could speak English," said Thomas, as he turned to Vin.

"Ask him what kind of experience he has had, and find out if any of his family are in the Army. See if he will tell you which side they're fighting on. It would be a real bitch to hire this guy and then find out his old man is the local V.C. Province Chief."

Quong spent the next hour answering questions put to him by both Vin and Captain Thomas. They asked about things he had heard of only from his cousin. What did he think about the Diem regimen? What were his feelings about the rash of self immolations by Buddhist monks? Quong was Buddhist himself, so he was surprised by the report of what the monks were doing to themselves.

"I think he is too simple to be lying, Dai Uy," said Vin, as they finished their lunch. They asked Quong to sketch the statue across the road as they talked, and he handed them a very good likeness on the back of the menu from the Carolina.

As Captain Thomas held the sketch, he turned to Vin. "Gut feeling, what do you think? We can use him if you think he's O.K." This was the beginning of Captain Thomas' second year in country, and he and Vin had been together the entire time. There was a close bond between them. Quong's fate was now in the hands, once again, of a stranger.

"We could put him in the G-3 shop and let him work for them in the chart branch. Who knows, you may want him to do some pictures of a statue to send home." Vin had given his approval.

"Tell him to get to the main gate of Ton Son Nhut. We can meet him there in the morning to get him in. Tell him if he screws up, I'll cut his nuts out and feed 'em to him."

Vin translated, verbatim.

Quong had a job in Saigon.

CHAPTER 3

Quong met Captain Thomas and Vin at the main entrance to the MACV annex at six a.m. the next morning. He was escorted to the Viet military police station for processing and clearance prior to his reporting to the G-3 section for a briefing on his duties.

"You must be here at 0700 each morning. You may leave at 1700. Sometimes you will work later and will have no prior notice. We will give you the tools you need to work with." The well dressed Vietnamese man briefing Quong did so without allowing the new employee to ask questions.

Another man standing beside Quong turned and asked, "Do you know what is meant by 0700 or 1700?

"No."

"Do you have a place to live in Saigon?" Quong was asked.

He realized he would have to find a place or live in the streets.

"No. I do not have a place. Do you know where I might stay?"

"I live in the Cong Li section. There is room for another if you would like to stay there. It will not cost you a lot of money and there is a place to cook. I will show you when we leave today."

"Good, I will follow you," Quong replied to his new-found friend.

"Now," said the man in charge, "I will escort you to your work area."

Throughout the compound men and women moved in all directions. Quong had no idea where this many people could be going all at one time. Although he was both impressed and awed at the activity, he knew instinctively that if he planned to function in this environment he must shed his country-boy awe and become a full-fledged member of this new society.

By late afternoon when he saw Captain Thomas again, Quong had been asked numerous questions about things which meant nothing to him. What were his political preferences? What religion did he practice? Had he ever helped the Viet Cong? Why was he not in the Army?

Quong could answer all but the questions regarding his military organization. He had never been in a position where he was required to join any military service. Would he join? Since there was no draft in Vietnam in 1964, he could accept or reject military service. At this point he decided to reject it. Two years later he found out a kidney defect would disqualify him permanently.

As he progressed in his job, he became more aware of the war and what it meant both now and for the future of his country. "If Vietnam is to survive, we will do so only with a great deal of American assistance," he told one of his co-workers at lunch one day. "Only if our people develop as individuals and take responsible positions in the rebirth of their country will we be able to exist without the Americans," he said.

Quong was doing his part. He was learning to read and write in his native language and was perfecting English as well. His job performance was beyond reproach. He did more than was asked of him and very soon made his way through the chain of command until he was in charge of all artists, or draftsmen as they were now called, on the MACV Plans and Operations staff. With this new duty came the added responsibility of providing charts and graphs for classified briefings. He was investigated for, and passed, a secret security clearance.

After two years of working for the Americans in Saigon, Quong brought his sister to the city. The plan was for her to find a job and send her wages home to Ap Binh Tay to their family. The two of them would live on Quong's money. The first job she found was working in a mess hall at the MACV compound. This satisfied the young girl for almost six months, but the sights and sounds of the ever increasing activity of Saigon were too much for her. She began to go out with the American servicemen, and less than one year after her arrival in Saigon, the dainty young girl from Ap Binh Tay became a live-in girl friend, a mistress for an American Army sergeant. It didn't stop with the sergeant. Many of the girls like Bea quickly developed a system. As one GI finished his twelve-month tour of duty and returned to the U.S., another would take his place. Quong spoke to his sister Bea frequently about her living arrangements, as he could not condone her actions. Although he was somewhat uncomfortable when around her, she was still his sister. His family ties were strong and not easily broken.

* * *

Quong awoke suddenly from a deep sleep. He had stayed up late the night before, celebrating with his sister. This was the season of the lunar year—Tet 1968. The pounding in his head was from more than the vast quantity of ba si da he had drunk. The potent rice wine was known for its delayed action but not like what he was feeling now.

Before he could regain his senses, his head and body were rocked by a violent explosion. For a fleeting instant he thought perhaps it was a large number of fireworks exploded by over-enthusiastic celebrants. The dust falling from the ceiling dispelled this theory. Quong knew this was no friendly Tet celebration.

The third explosion threw him onto the floor of the small two-room house in which he had lived for the last two years. His home was in a good location for him. The house was not far from the Chorlon Race Track and was only one block from the main highway leading to MACV. Work was less than an hour ride by bicycle for him.

The Chorlon Race Track provided many hours of entertainment for Quong, who had recently developed a passion for betting. On occasion, especially during some of the frequent holidays they celebrated, he and Bea spent a day there.

The racetrack now provided an excellent point of reference and staging ground for the Viet Cong who had been planning this offensive for months.

After seven days and the loss of thousands of lives, both Viet Cong and South Viet, the racetrack was recaptured and the last VC defender killed. Only then was Quong able to make it back to his job at MACV.

Things were never the same for Quong, Bea or Vietnam after Tet 1968.

As the war effort began to draw down, the Americans began the process called Vietnamization. The official policy was to let the Viets fight their own war. With this philosophy in place, the Viets who worked with the Americans took on a more active and important role. Quong was no exception, as his importance increased to the point where he was producing maps of Viet Cong and NVA locations based on information provided by prisoners and Chieu Hois.

During 1971, Quong realized his country was almost surely losing the war. Large numbers of Americans were being pulled out of his country, and the fighting was being turned over to a less than dedicated fighting force. From his perspective, it was the local troops, the Regional Forces and Popular forces—Ruff Puff, the Americans called them—who were fighting to win the war. Unfortunately, they alone could not do it.

The dark days of the spring of 1975 came like the apex of an earthquake. Quong had felt the rumbles of the oncoming destruction for several years. After the American POWs were returned, the ground began to shake and crumble in earnest. Quong and Bea packed as much as they could in two small bags, climbed aboard his motorcycle and, like thousands of other South Vietnamese, fled the horror of Saigon.

The highway they selected went south toward their old family home. Along the way they met refugees going in both directions. Many felt they could melt into the crowds of Saigon. Others wanted to get as far away as possible from the new center of government. Many were simply running.

About fifty kilometers south of Saigon, Quong found out how desperate some of these people were. While slowing his cycle to almost a crawl around the mass of people in the highways and along the roadside, Quong saw two men arguing over a metal can containing gasoline they both wanted for their motorcycles.

"I want your extra can of gasoline. I will pay you for it." A middle-aged man waived a handful of piasters at a young man who was unimpressed with the money. "I can even give a small piece of gold for it," he said as he reached across in an attempt to grab the can which was secured by a piece of rope.

"It is not for sale. For piasters, for gold, for anything." The owner attempted to pull around the man blocking his path.

"I must have the gasoline. I can go no further without it," he said angrily. Midway through his shouting and arm waving, the older of the two men calmly, and with total disregard to everyone and everything around them, pulled a pistol from the waist band of his pants and shot the other in the head.

Few people seemed to notice what had happened. Before the blood had ceased running from the fatal wound, two other men pushed the dead man's motorcycle over to a small two wheeled cart where they produced enough gasoline to fill its tank. Once filled, the men and their new motorcycle melted into the crowd.

Quong and Bea came to their first manned roadblock about two miles northeast of the Province capital city of An Bac.

Quong slowed his cycle to a creep as he pulled in behind the line of some twenty or more people waiting for the guard's permission to proceed.

"Where are you going?" asked the guard, as he casually emphasized his sentence by pointing the barrel of the Russian made AK-47 assault rifle at the two people on the cycle.

"We're going home to rejoin our family. We've been away so long it's difficult to imagine that things could have been destroyed by the Americans and our ex-countrymen who sided with them." It hurt Quong to speak in this manner, but under the circumstances it was necessary.

"We've been living and working in Da Lat. Have you ever been there?" he asked the guard.

"No, but my brother passed through there on his way to Hue. He says it is beautiful."

"Perhaps now you will be able to visit. Our people will soon have it fully functional as a city once again." As he spoke, Quong was slowly inching forward until he had to yell over his shoulder to finish his conversation with the guard.

Once back in his native village of Ap Binh Tay, life went on as it had for decades. The main objective in life was survival. There was rice to plant and harvest, fish to catch and prepare and an occasional trip to market. For reasons known only to Quong and his sister, the two of them stayed very close to the tiny hamlet.

Bea was the fist to venture out. She went on a taxi boat trip up the Song Bay river to the largest city in An Bac Province. With the exception of political indoctrination classes conducted throughout the city and two compounds for political prisoners, there was no great change in the day-to-day activities of the people in the city. Even during the war, most of the civilian population had been more than content to let the war happen around them. If there was a great silent majority in Vietnam, the people of An Bac's capitol city represented it quite nicely.

Bea's first objective was to find a job. She knew hard work from her time spent in the struggle to exist in her old village. She also knew the good life. She had worn western clothes and had luxuries such as a television, air conditioner, stereo and nice jewelry while in Saigon. These things had been either sold or left behind when she fled the city. To regain even some of them now would be a fulfillment of an almost impossible dream.

In order to maintain a low profile in the capitol city of Vu Boi, she had to completely—and with great care—ignore anyone whom she might know. This was not a difficult task since others felt the same way, and few people on the streets or in the marketplace of Vu Boi wished to be recognized by anyone from their pre-communist past.

It took less than three days for the simple farm girl, who carried herself with a great amount of dignity, to find a job. It was not the type of job she would have accepted under normal conditions, but these were times of great turmoil for everyone.

Bea got a job in a military compound on the northern edge of the city. Just as in Saigon, her first job was as a cook.

For three months her family and friends in Ap Binh Tay did not hear from Bea. One day a hand-written note was delivered to Quong by a friend returning from the district market place by taxi-boat.

It was a brief note telling everyone Bea had found work and was doing well. The last line was intended only for Quong. He did not completely understand its meaning but he knew his sister well enough to give her full credibility. The note said simply, "There is much for you here. Come quickly, but do not plan to stay."

"Father, I must talk to you. I would like to join you at the spirit house tonight." Quong's request was understood as a plea to his father.

The two men met at dusk at the spirit house behind their home. The little structure, only slightly larger than a bird house, was the center of their religious activities. Here they offered incense and fruit for Buddha.

They bowed in the traditional fashion, palms together in front of their faces, and offered their gifts to Buddha.

"Once again I must leave Ap Binh Tay. I will see Bea in Vu Boi." Quong did not look at his father as he spoke. "Bea has asked for me. I feel I must go."

"Many things have changed since you left before," his father said. "One thing that has not or will not change is the family. Remember, I am old and you are soon to be the head of the family. You must do what is right for the family. I give Bea to you, Quong. My daughter is now yours."

If their incense burned completely and the fruit shriveled and rotted, it showed Buddha was pleased. They would know their offering was accepted and the prayer would be fulfilled. This was their belief, simple, but it fulfilled their needs. Buddha, like Quong, needed time to react.

Morning in the Mekong brought hot steamy weather with first light. Quong was used to this, so he arose with no difficulty, packed a few personal items in a small canvas bag and began the long walk along the rice paddy dikes up river to the district market. There he would catch one of the long flat-bottom sampans going further up river to Vu Boi where he would meet his sister. Since returning from Saigon, this was the first time Quong had dared venture out to a city as large or important as Vu Boi.

Once he arrived at the district town, it took less than an hour to find a boat going to Vu Boi. Not willing to part with cash for passage, Quong agreed to work by unloading and helping pole the boat up river. During the war there would have been no need to pole since most of the boats had small gasoline engines. Now with gas in short supply, even at outrageous prices on the black market, few could afford gas for motors. Most had simply reverted back to poles or the long sweeping rudder which, when used properly, could propel a boat almost as fast as some of the smaller engines.

Quong had little difficulty finding his sister. She had said in her letter she was living across from the old American airfield. The small landing strip was on the outskirts of town next to the one and only highway in the capitol city. During the war the area would have been full of traffic. Now it was almost deserted except for people on foot or bicycles.

"This is a nice place in which you live," said Quong as his sister greeted him in the one room she rented. "I see you have managed to accumulate a few nice things." Quong spoke as he walked around the room, examining a large black chest and an electric fan. "Can you use this?"

"The electricity is turned on one hour each evening. That is when the political classes are given and radio broadcasts are made. So far I have not been required to attend any classes, but we must listen to the radio each evening. To do otherwise would be to ask for trouble."

"There are too many things here for one person. Do you have someone living with you?" Quong's voice dropped as he turned to face his sister. "Or do you live with someone yourself?"

"I am a grown woman, Quong. I do what I must in order to survive. Now as before. Do not be so quick to judge me. It is not as it may appear."

"Who is this person? Is he a shop keeper in Vu Boi? A farmer? How does he keep you?"

"He works at the compound where I am a cook. His name is Minh," she said as she stood and walked to the open front door. Bea looked down the once paved road, now filled with craters and holes. "Minh should be coming home at any time."

"Is he a cook also?"

Bea stood with her back to Quong. "No, he's a guard. He---"

"A guard! You're living with the Viet Cong!" Before he could continue with his outburst, Bea turned and covered his mouth with her hand.

"Don't be a fool! To yell in disrespect like that is to ask for certain trouble." She spoke in a harsh whisper as she quickly and almost forcefully pushed Quong into the far corner of the room.

"They are not the Viet Cong now. They are the government. The leaders of our country. To be heard talking against them now would be like speaking out against the GVN in 1970. You don't have to agree with them. You can disagree with them and their policy, but it is very dangerous to do so aloud. But that is not why I asked you here. I want you to meet and talk to Minh while we eat, and then you and I will go for a walk. I have something I wish to tell you. I don't want anyone else to hear us."

Throughout their meal of rice and dried shrimp mixed with hot red pepper and other spices, Quong spoke infrequently to Minh. Even so, there was something about the simple man's attitude that Quong felt drawn to. It was not an instant liking or appreciation but rather a recognition that, like Quong and his sister, Minh was a survivor.

After dinner Minh prepared for his one luxury, a nightly bottle of 33 beer. The warm beer was usually consumed during the hour all radios were required to be on as the political broadcast beamed throughout the Delta each evening.

Since the broadcast was also played on loudspeakers placed throughout the city, the locals could leave their homes without fear of drawing attention to themselves. This was the time Bea selected for the two of them to walk from her house to the central market district.

"What is this important matter you wish to discuss?" asked Quong as soon as they were away from the house.

"Quong, I know how you feel about me, but do not let this anger with me change your trust in what I am about to tell you."

"I have seen Americans living in the compound where

Minh and I work. I cook for them and twice they have come into the main area to eat. Minh guards one who is held by himself. These are Americans, Quong! They were not released as POWs. I have given it much thought since I found out about them, and I feel this information would be worth a great deal of money to the Americans."

"I know many people are escaping to other countries, especially the United States. If one or both of us could go and tell Americans, I'm sure we would be rewarded. What do you think?"

"I think your plan is admirable; however, I question your motives and objective. It is one thing to make a living from the Americans in Saigon, but to sell them information about POWs is quite another."

"Don't be so simple," she cautioned. "We will be stuck in this wretched place forever unless we make a move. You had no hesitation about leaving once. Why must you do so now?"

Quong walked beside Bea in silence. As he passed the many vendors in the central marketplace, he saw in the shops remnants of the Americans' presence there and the good life—by Vietnamese standard—that he and his sister had lived during the war. Some of the shops still had radios, cameras, fans and other items considered necessities a few years ago. These same items on today's black market commanded prices few people could pay.

On front of one shop, now closed, was a full length mirror. The place had at one time been a tailor shop owned by Indians or Pakistanis who came to Vietnam in the mid-'60s. These people opened shops throughout the country, made their money, then left. This shop had been closed for many years. Nothing of any value remained, with the exception of the large mirror affixed to the outer wall.

The two of them stopped at the doorway. For several silent minutes Quong studied the reflected image of the two of them in the mirror. The silent man and his sister were beginning to show irreversible damage from the life they were now leading. They were both underweight, though nowhere near starvation. Bea was dressed in the traditional ao dao rather than a skirt as she preferred. Quong had long since worn out the last pair of jeans which he so dearly loved to wear, and today wore only thin cotton pants, a shirt, and a pair of well worn and repaired sandals.

Perhaps, he thought, with this information of Bea's they could live better in America.

Quong spoke to his sister. "I do not think the Americans would simply take my word on a matter like this. We would need proof. And how would I or we get there, to America?" As Quong spoke his voice reflected his enthusiasm.

"Perhaps I have already worked out the details of the solution to some of these problems," said Bea as she took her brother by the hand and started the walk back to her house.

CHAPTER 4

For the men and women who had been to both places, the comparison between the weather in Vietnam and Georgia in the summer was immediately and sometimes painfully evident.

Like the heat of Vietnam, the summer brought days of high temperatures and equally high humidity, leaving everything and everybody in it drenched in minutes. Unlike Vietnam, the men and women in Georgia didn't have the advantage of wearing the cool, loose-fitting jungle fatigues issued in the war zone. Here the uniform was a prescribed regimentation that sometimes included a coat and tie.

Just as in Vietnam, the weather was an enemy. There were as many heat strokes and heat-related injuries at the military posts in Georgia in summer as in Vietnam.

It was here, in the heat and humidity, that the army established a number of small, quick, training and orientation courses designed for men, and occasionally a few women, enroute to Vietnam.

The Joint Military Intelligence Committee Headquarters was established at Fort McCullars, Georgia, but not for these reasons. It was placed here because there was an office building on the post which was not being used.

The offices of the Joint Military Intelligence Committee were located in a small brick building on the Fort. Few people other than those assigned there knew or cared about the day-to-day operation of the clearinghouse for intelligence data for all the U.S. military services. The location was ideal. There was a military recruiting command headquarters also housed at the post. These two commands had people of all services working there so as to provide easy cover, if necessary, to dispel any questions about the variety of uniforms worn by those assigned there.

The collection, evaulation and dissemination of useful intelligence data from all over the world was the main function of this headquarters; however, those working there also picked up additional duties and missions as in any other military unit. One of these was the investigation of reports on American POW sightings in Vietnam, Cambodia and Laos.

Since Asian refugees had begun arriving from Vietnam, more than three hundred POW sightings had been reported. Of these, less than twenty had been placed in open, active files by J.M.I. Even though these sightings remained in an active file, there was little hope anything would or could be done about them. That was the official position of the United States government and its military components; the men and women of J.M.I. did not necessarily support this policy. Each report was worked with enthusiasm, since there was an outside chance that it might prove factual. What to do if it did, posed a problem they had not yet officially broached.

Today, Karl Jensen signed for the morning dispatches. These included the electronically transmitted messages from other agencies which came in overnight.

"You've got a meeting with the boss at 0930, sir," said

the Air Force sergeant as he waited for Jensen to finish verifying the number of messages. "From what Major Dixon said, it's just a routine briefing. You know the old man's finally going on leave, so he probably wants to police up the battlefield prior to leaving." The last part was a reference to one of the boss's favorite pet sayings.

"Gentlemen, the Commander." Navy Captain Bill Smith, the second-in-command, called the assembled officers to their feet in a voice that boomed several decibels louder than necessary.

"Please, take your seats. This won't take long. As most of you know, I'm going on leave tomorrow, so I want to police up the battlefield before I go." As he spoke Major General Tom Burkhalter slid easily into his seat at the head of the table.

Burkhalter had a long and distinguished career within the military intelligence community. He started his first intelligence mission by operating behind enemy lines deep within what is now North Korea, during 1951-52. Prior to that he had been an enlisted man in WWII. His subsequent assignments had taken him from the jungles of South America to mountaintops in Turkey and West Germany. He had assisted in the initial planning and operation of the Phoenix Program in South Vietnam. His credentials in the intelligence field were flawless, and he demanded the same in his staff. Integrity, loyalty and professionalism were expected—and received.

"Most of the dispatches are fairly routine," he observed, as he quickly read through the traffic from the previous night. "Does anyone have anything earth-shattering?" the General joked with his staff.

"Just one thing, sir," Jensen slid a short message across the table to him. "This came in as I was coming down here to the briefing."

Burkhalter recognized the form immediately. It was one

used for reports of U.S. POWs.

This one was over two pages long.

"This one seems interesting, sir; it's from the World Refugee Organization in Malaysia. They've got a Vietnamese national who just made it in from Vietnam. He's reported a sighting in An Bac, down in the Delta." Lieutenant Colonel Jensen waited for Burkhalter and Captain Smith to read the report.

"This guy's done his homework. He claims to have worked for us at MACV in Saigon. Said he held a secret clearance. World Refugee didn't have his name, but he talked a pretty good game so they segregated him from the others. They're awaiting guidance from us now."

As refugees began to escape from Vietnam, a makeshift clearinghouse had been quickly put together in Malaysia since this was where most of the anticipated thousands of men and women would land. The operation was placed under the control of the World Refugee Organization. This multinational group gave it the best cover.

A list of personnel who worked with the U.S. government and its military forces was then compiled. This list included names of ranking military, province and district political leaders, Phoenix operatives, and a miscellaneous assortment of other personnel who had been loyal to the U.S. and the Saigon regime. Many Viets were placed on the list because of the security clearance which they held. The majority of the names on the list could be eliminated since the people had not or would not arrive.

As the people on the list appeared at the refugee centers, they were given preferential treatment and expedited to re-settlement centers in the U.S. or countries which agreed to take them. Because of this, it became known as the expedite list. "Did he show up on the expedite list?" asked the J.M.I. Senior Naval Officer, Captain Smith, as he finished reading his copy of the printed form.

"With only a secret clearance it's doubtful he would, but as you can see in the message the people in Malaysia recommend further interrogation. He must have told them something they're not putting in writing. There's a courier flight coming through Singapore on Tuesday. We can have him on it and in here by Friday morning." There was a hint of excitement in Jensen's voice as he spoke of the possibility of personally interviewing one of the numerous people who reported sightings.

"You want to give it a shot, Bill?"

Burkhalter was leaving the decision up to his deputy.

"Let's give him a look-see. We've got a fairly light case load. We only have about twenty sightings still open in our files. Maybe he'll be able to clear up some of them."

Without waiting for further instructions, Smith turned to the two officers seated across from him and began to issue instructions to them. "Karl, get him on the courier flight. He's your responsibility. You're in charge of care and feeding. Major Dixon, see if we have his name on file. If he had a secret clearance, maybe Defense Intelligence has something in the files. That's about all we can do based on what we now have. Maybe we'll have more to work with when he gets here."

With J.M.I. having so many areas of responsibility in the world, and the variety of intelligence agencies reporting to them, there was little time for speculation about Quong and his claim until he was actually there and they talked to him.

"Got a minute, sir?" Tom Dixon stood in the doorway to Captain Smith's office. "I've got an update on our expedite refugee. I've verified his clearance through Naval Intelligence. N.I.L.O. did his investigation in Saigon. I've even got a fingerprint card coming. He worked at the MACV annex in Saigon in the J-3 section. When we pulled out he must have gone back into the bush."

"He should be here tomorrow. Jensen verified he got him manifested for the courier flight. He'll lay over at Travis and get in here tomorrow morning. It shouldn't take long to find out if he's blowing smoke." Smith rose from behind his desk as he spoke to Dixon. "I've got a court reserved at 1300. You feel like some racketball?"

Dixon knew this was more than a request. Few people made the mistake of appearing at Smith's door just before he went to the racketball courts. Even at his age Smith was deadly on the court.

Captain Bill Smith was a mustang. He started his service with the Navy a month prior to the North Korean invasion of South Korea. He distinguished himself in the first operation in which he participated. It was a personal recommendation by Admiral George Rhodes that got Smith his direct commission.

Since that time, the lean, slightly balding man had taken on the job of keeping the United States Navy and its sister services' intelligence community informed when he felt they had a need to know. Every scrap of information, every detail of the thousands of memos, reports and dispatches he read over the twenty-odd years had been neatly filed in his computer-like memory bank, ready for instant recall as needed.

Like many military men, he had traded his family for his career. His wife of thirteen years left him and took their two children with her. If there was anything that meant more to him than his career, it was his children. Although he was unable to express it at the time, he could now look back on their years together and see his mistakes. Being able to see personal mistakes and taking steps to change them presented a challenge that he was not always able to accept.

The two men finished their game and returned directly to the office. Lunch was a luxury Smith did not often allow himself.

The remainder of the afternoon passed uneventfully. By the time the office workers began their trek to the many small bedroom communities surrounding Ft. McCullars, there was barely a break in the heat of the Georgia afternoon. Even the walk from an air-conditioned office to a car in the adjacent parking lot was enough to bring a person to a full sweat. The humidity and heat were factors one either despised with a passion or accepted as facts of life. There was no middle ground, no neutrality in this matter.

Smith went to his quarters on post. Jensen met his wife and young son for dinner at a local steak house, and Tom Dixon drove to his house where his wife Beth had dinner almost ready.

"That you, Tom?" she called from the kitchen as she heard their front door open.

"You were expecting the Jolly Green Giant?" he joked as he strode into the kitchen and gave his wife a quick kiss.

"While I finish dinner, why don't you change and go get Smokey. I'd like to ride him after a while."

Tom had trained their horse Smokey to come to the gate at the rear of their house whenever he whistled. Each time he did this he always took an apple or carrot or some other treat for the horse. Beth was unable to call Smokey in this manner, for no matter how hard she tried she could not whistle.

Apple in hand, Tom moved across the back deck down the steps and walked to the fence. One loud whistle and Smokey shortly appeared at a rise midway across the ten acre pasture.

At this point, Smokey usually began to run, criss-crossing the pasture as he came down the hill. This usually made Beth stop her activities and watch the horse as he crashed down the pasture, black mane flying.

Beth's after-dinner ride left Tom alone and gave him time to think about the next day's activities.

* * *

The morning sun split the darkness of the eastern sky with a promise of sufficient heat to create another soul-drenching day in central Georgia.

Most of the men and women assigned to J.M.I. and the other commands at McCullars arrived in their individual autos and massed carpools prior to 0730. By that time, the J.M.I. duty officer had already picked up the overnight dispatches and delivered them to Lieutenant Colonel Jensen's office.

Major Dixon came in early to cover for Jensen since he was to pick up the Viet refugee from the courier flight at 0655. As of his arrival in the office at 0710, Dixon had not heard from Jensen.

"Morning, Sir," said Dixon as he and Captain Smith met at the coffee maker in the utility room.

"You should've been there last night, Tom." Smith filled his large heavy ceramic mug with the first of his many doses of strong black coffee. They've got a new large screen T.V. at the club. We watched Atlanta and San Francisco play a pre-season game. If they can keep the injuries down, they both are going to have one hell of a season." Smith stopped talking long enough to sip the hot steaming coffee. "Have you heard from Jensen? Has he picked up the Viet yet?"

"Good morning Captain. Tom." The resonant voice of Lieutenant Colonel Jensen greeted the two men as they emerged, cups in hand.

"Have you got him, Karl? I don't mind telling you I'm a little excited about having one of these guys down here with us. Did he say anything during the ride in from the airport?" Captain Smith, like the others, was beginning to feel the excitement of what could lay ahead.

"Not a word. He's clammed up tighter than Dick's hat band. The guys on the courier flight said the only time he spoke to them was when they hit some rough weather and he barfed his cookies over Guam. I've got him down in my office. Lieutenant Moore is looking out for him. He wanted breakfast on the way in so I picked up some stuff. He should be finished by now."

"O.K., guys, let's do it. Let's go see what this one can tell us that we haven't heard before." Smith led the way.

Midway down the hall he stopped and turned to Dixon. "I know you guys took a crash course in Vietnamese during Special Forces training. Do I have to rely on you as interpreters or can he speak English?"

"From what I can tell, his English is pretty good. Colonel Jensen said he knows how to order bacon and eggs and a can of beer for chow. That made me feel right at home."

Quong rose quickly from his seat behind Jensen's desk as the three men entered. He moved around to stand almost at attention in front of the large grey metal desk as Jensen introduced the two men to him.

As each was introduced, Quong repeated their name in English and when a handshake was offered he took the man's hand in both of his and bowed slightly in a show of respect. The act was obviously sincere. Smith and Dixon were both impressed by his genuine display of respect.

"Mr. Quong, I want you to finish your food and, if necessary, take an hour or so to relax. When you are rested a bit we can talk about the information you have for us." Smith was choosing his words carefully. He did not want the Vietnamese to pick up anything misleading from the words or tone of his voice.

"Captain, I am ready to tell you now about what I know in Vietnam. Much time has already gone. The man I have seen should not wait even one minute while I rest or eat, for he is not allowed to do either."

Both Jensen and Dixon knew this was an attitude Smith could relate to.

"Mr. Quong, if you don't mind, there are a few personal questions I would like to ask you prior to your telling us about your spotting of American POWs." Smith led Quong into a small conference room across the hall from Jensen's office.

Once inside, Quong sat easily in a large, brown-cushioned straight-back chair. The table in front of him was built for people much taller than his small five-foot, four-inch frame, so he looked much like a large child sitting there.

Rather than take a seat, Smith quickly sat on the edge of the table facing Quong. In front of Smith lay the open folder, with copies of the limited amount of data on the Viet which the men had been able to accumulate and have electronically transmitted to their headquarters.

The folder was opened and placed in such a way that Quong was well aware of the contents. He could not tell specifically what each document was, but he could recognize them as pertaining to him.

"My Vietnamese is a little rusty, so forgive me if I try it and mispronounce anything," Smith began. "According to what I have here, you should be thirty-seven now."

"My age is now thirty-eight. My birthdate is 24 August," Quong corrected.

The three Americans smiled, each knowing the little man in their midst had just passed the first of many subtle—and not so subtle—tests which were to be given him.

For over an hour the men went through a session bordering on an interrogation. Quong answered each question when asked. At one point he asked for a pen and paper and drew a sketch of the office building in the MACV annex in which he worked. Dixon was the only one of the Americans who had been there so he verified the accuracy of the sketch.

At one point Quong became frustrated with what appeared to him to be somewhat petty questioning. Captain Smith sensed this and called a short break in the interview.

Quong was escorted down the hallway to the men's room as the three others went behind closed doors in Smith's office.

"O.K., what do you guys think? Give me a gut feeling. Is he for real?" Smith stood in front of the two men. He had one hand in his pocket, jingling his keys in nervous response to the current situation.

"He's right on top of what he's told us so far. I don't think he's missed a strike." Jensen turned to Dixon. "What do you think, Tom? You were at MACV for a while. Do you see any holes in his story?"

"So far it looks good. He even drew in the clearance area at the annex in the sketch. Viet Nationals weren't even allowed in that area without a Secret Code. It sure looks good so far."

"Let's go see if he wants to talk about POWs. That's what he's here for. Tom, get a C.I.D. agent in here to fingerprint him and compare it with the card we have. So far he hasn't shown any signs of jet lag or being tired. Let's push him a bit. See if he's looking for a free ride or what." The excitement had turned to cool professional determination in Smith. "If he's for real, I want to find out in a hurry. We don't have time to screw around with some Vietnamese who's looking for a free ride. Or for that matter with one that's got a hard on for us because he thinks we left him behind when the U.S. pulled out. None of us have time for those games."

Almost as an afterthought, and half aloud to the other two, he added, "I don't know why I want to hurry. If he is for real, if he can give us a location, what the hell do we do with it?"

Neither man answered.

CHAPTER 5

As he reentered the world of the Americans, Quong thought back to his days with MACV in Saigon.

"I know these men," he thought to himself as he walked down the hallway. "I have seen them or ones like them in my own country." With this in the back of his mind, Quong knew he was now in a good position with the three American officers. He had worked for Americans long enough in Saigon to almost type-cast them. Even though they were working as a team, Quong saw a distinct difference between the three men with whom he would now spend so much time.

Smith was the leader, not only by virtue of his rank but by his demeanor. The way he acted and reacted was a sign to Quong that the cool, calculating man was totally in charge.

Lieutenant Colonel Karl Jensen was aloof, pushy. He tried too hard. Quong was certain that during the questioning session, Jensen had been trying to impress Smith as much as he was trying to get information. Quong would have to watch him carefully. There were few Karl Jensens in Vietnamese society.

There was an almost instant mutual respect between

Quong and Tom Dixon, the Army major. Since his arrival at J.M.I. Headquarters, the two of them had been drawn to each other. In the few short hours of their acquaintance, they had shared bits of conversation like two long lost friends.

"I will spend a lot of time with you, Quong. If you need anything, let me know." Dixon had spoken slowly and quietly to Quong. It was not a condescending tone, but rather a way to ensure Quong understood.

"I have few needs at this time, Major, but I thank you for asking." Quong recognized the sincerity of Dixon's words and actions.

The major was impressive to Quong in many ways. To the newly arrived Vietnamese refugee, the American represented the power Quong had once known in his native country. His uniform, his military bearing and the way he presented himself to his senior told Quong he was a man who could be both a professional soldier and a true friend. Quong hoped he would see both sides of the man prior to the end of their association if such an end did, in fact, take place.

For a while Quong felt somewhat ill at ease around these Americans. He was afraid of their reaction to the almost shabby manner in which he was dressed. Since landing in Malaysia he had worn only the clothing furnished him by the World Refugee Organization. He arrived at their resettlement camp in a pair of shorts and sandals. The shirt he started the journey with simply came apart after two weeks at sea. The remainder of his personal items, including his clothing, had been stolen by raiding pirates.

He now wore a pair of loose fitting brown slacks and a long-sleeved white shirt with the sleeves rolled up to his elbows. The remainder of the personal items which had been given to him by World Refugee were placed in an

AWOL bag that he kept by his side at all times. His only request when he arrived in Malaysia had been for a piece of thin leather thong about two feet long. He had asked for, and been given, a leather boot lace. This he tied loosely around his neck. It wasn't like the gold chain Bea had given him, but it would do for now.

The three men had all but abandoned the normal activities of their jobs with J.M.I. when Quong arrived. Fortunately, the other men and women assigned there could take up any slack caused by the absence of these men. Everyone, out of operational necessity, could back up any other member of the staff.

Quong could sense the tension in the air as the men settled themselves for what he knew was to be the beginning of the real questioning period. Even he realized that up until now they had been testing for soft spots. It was similar to the American practice of using artillery to soften an area prior to sending in the infantry.

The artillery fire had ceased and been lifted, the gunships were circling and, for Quong, the combat assault was about to begin. In his mind, Quong could almost smell and taste the sulphur-based gunpowder and cordite hanging heavy in the air.

Captain Smith took the initiative when the men entered the room. "Quong," said Smith as he eliminated the "Mister" he had previously used when he addressed the man, "I would like to tape what you say for the remainder of the afternoon." Without waiting for an answer, he placed a small silver tape recorder on the table between the men. It was battery operated with a built-in microphone; therefore, there was no clutter on the large table top.

"I want to be perfectly honest with you, Quong." Smith leaned forward across the end of the table as he spoke. "I'm sure you realize there have been many reports of Americans still in Vietnam. You can also appreciate the dilemma we find ourselves in. We can't simply hop on a plane and go have a look-see for ourselves. I don't think we would be too welcome. So, this being the case, tell us about the American you saw."

The cold manner in which Smith addressed him caught Quong slightly off guard. If this was the way things were to be presented from now on, Quong knew he could handle his part of the program. He felt the man would be professional; but even judging him by how some of the Americans in Saigon acted, he was abrupt and too quick.

Quong took his time. He shifted in his seat, bringing himself to his full height as he sat facing the senior officer. He folded his hands and placed them in front of him on the table. He could feel the sweat begin to mist upon his forehead as a nervous reaction to the situation. He was sure the blood flowing through his veins at unheard of speeds was causing the leather thong around his neck to jump and jerk in spasms as the skin gave way to the surges. Fortunately, the bottom end of the leather loop was well inside his shirt and out of view. This was his "ace in the hole" as he often heard his American friends in Saigon say, and he was not yet ready to play it.

"Dai Ta, Trung Ta, Tieu Ta," Quong addressed each man in the Vietnamese equivalent of his rank. I do not care that others have told of POWs. I have no knowledge of these men. Perhaps someone else has told of the men in An Bac. I know only what I have seen with my own eyes." By now Quong was beginning to raise his voice ever so slightly. He was clenching and unclenching his hands into fists as he talked. None of these actions went unnoticed by the three Americans.

"I left my home less than three months ago. The information I give you is fresh. The North Vietnamese running the compound where your man is do not even know me, and my sister Bea is the only person to miss me. I can tell you where this man is." Quong leaned forward, almost in an imitation of Captain Smith. "And I can show you how to rescue him."

With these last words Quong leaned back, crossed his arms across his chest and, with a smug, almost impish half grin on his face, waited for his words to sink in.

He didn't have long to wait.

"Quong," said Jensen, "I'm sure you know what you're telling us is extremely important. We can't simply take it at surface value nor, unfortunately, can we confirm or substantiate it to the degree we would like. We're going to spend quite a bit of time together for the next few days, so I want you to think very carefully as we talk. Try to recall in detail as much as you can about the area where you say you've seen the American.

While Jensen was talking to Quong, Major Dixon slid a note across the table to Smith. When Smith unfolded the yellow-lined note he read it and nodded his agreement to Dixon's written suggestion that they notify the Chairman of the J.M.I., Major General Tom Burkhalter, and ask him to come by prior to departing for leave.

Dixon got up from the table and exited the room before Jensen finished talking to Quong. Like a stonefaced oriental statue, Quong listened to Jensen without emotion or words.

Major Dixon closed the door to his office as he entered. He picked up his telephone, dialed one number and heard a second dial tone which indicated he was now plugged into the civilian phone system. He quickly dialed the number to Burkhalter's quarters. After three rings a woman's voice responded, "Burkhalter's residence."

"Mrs. Burkhalter, this is Major Dixon. I hate to bother you this afternoon, but I really need to talk to the General if he's around."

"You can talk to him on one condition, Tom. When he hangs up I still want to be on leave and going to Florida this evening. You wouldn't deprive me the pleasure of going to Disney World would you?"

After almost thirty years of marriage to a man who had spent his entire life in the military, a wife had little choice in matters such as this. She learned to expect cancelled plans, missed birthdays and anniversaries,and two-day field problems that lasted two weeks. Even so, Tom could tell she was only half joking when she gave him the ground rules.

"You know I wouldn't do anything to disrupt your vacation, Mrs. Burkhalter. All of us at the office are looking forward to the General relaxing a bit. Maybe he'll even bring us an autographed picture of Mickey Mouse."

"O.K. Stand by. I'll get him."

"Hello, Tom, what's going on?" Burkhalter was almost gruff. It was as if he anticipated the call from someone at J.M.I. and what it was sure to mean.

"Sir, you remember the Vietnamese we had coming to us by way of the World Refugee Organization? Well, we've got him in the conference room with Captain Smith and Lieutenant Colonel Jensen. He's coming on like gang busters. Captain Smith wants to give you a chance to see him prior to your going on leave. We've been pushing since early morning. I think he's about to hit his burn-out factor. If you want to come by we will back off 'til you arrive."

While Dixon was speaking, Burkhalter, as was his custom, did not interrupt. The man let others speak until they were through and then he unloaded his questions.

"Does Smitty think I need to see him?" He emphasized the word "need." "Have you found out any information we didn't know already? Did anything come in on him to back up any of his claims to working for us in Saigon?"

"We confirmed he did work at MACV in Saigon. We've got a CID agent coming in to print him and compare it to a fingerprint card we found in his file. He should be here at any time. Sir," Dixon hesitated, "I hate to do this to you and Mrs. B but I think you should at least stop by."

"All right, Tom. Tell Smitty I'll be there in an hour. Get everything together for me. We'll see what he looks like when I get there."

The marathon session was beginning to take its toll on Quong. The jet lag and the intensity with which they were firing questions at him was causing him to slow down in his response time. On two occasions he had reverted to his native Vietnamese language when answering a question. The act had been instantaneous and happened without Quong even noticing it. Both times Dixon had to ask him to repeat his answer in English.

The men stopped their questioning when General Burkhalter arrived at the headquarters.

"Tom, take Quong out for a few minutes. I'll bet it's been quite some time since he's had a Coke. Why don't you take him down to the snack bar and get him one." Smith spoke to Major Dixon as he picked up the long, yellow, legal pad on which he had been writing notes and prepared to meet Burkhalter in the General's office.

"Karl, see that no one comes in here while we're out. Check on that CID man. I want a check on Quong's prints before we pack it in tonight."

Quong and Dixon left together.

"When you were in Vietnam, what did you do? Were you with an American unit or were you a co van?" asked Quong using the Vietnamese word for advisor.

It was the first time since the two of them met earlier in the day that they were alone.

"Toi la nguoi my." Dixon used the opportunity to answer Quong in his own language.

The smile which immediately appeared on Quong's face was an instant indication that Dixon's Vietnamese was still understandable after years of inactivity; and Quong, like so many of his countrymen, was impressed with an American who took the time and effort to master the difficult language.

As they entered the large room full of vending machines, Quong was immediately taken by surprise at the vast number of mechanical giants dispensing everything from gum to pizza.

Slowly, with a curiosity like the day he first arrived in Saigon so many years ago, Quong walked cautiously up to the closest machine. Inside small glass enclosures, like animals in a zoo, a variety of meals prepared in aluminum pouches, plates and trays were on view. Many were recognizable to Quong from the picture of the item placed next to the selection button. Others were as foreign to him as would be his native dishes to most of the people seated around the room.

"Never in Vietnam did I see so many machines with so much to choose from. Once in front of P.X. at Ton Son Nhut Air Base I saw three machines, but never so many as here. How do you know which to choose?" As he talked, Quong moved around the room touching first one then another machine, stopping occasionally to peer into the window at an item.

"You soon learn what not to eat from these. It's easier to keep up that way." The two men laughed as even Quong understood the wisdom of Dixon's statement.

Quong purchased a Coke. The familiar red and white can tumbled through the insides of the machine to make its way to Quong's waiting hands, as his childlike curiosity was captured by an item in the adjacent vendor.

"Is this a special type? I have enjoyed this many times in Vietnam but it was always much larger than this. I think this is not very much to eat." Quong was bending down peering into a display window. There was a question in his voice that could be answered in only one way.

"I think you may enjoy this, Quong." Dixon fumbled in his pocket until he produced enough change to feed into the machine.

Once satisfied the correct change was in its mechanical heart—or so it seemed to Quong—the monster allowed him to open the door and extract a small flat silver package about five inches square.

"I'll show you another miracle of American technology." Quong handed the small silver packet to Dixon who pulled off a paper wrapper and placed it face up in a microwave. After closing the door, Dixon turned the top dial and pressed one button.

"Now, Quong, keep your eye on the packet." As Dixon spoke, Quong had already leaned down to eye level with the glass door, totally unprepared for what happened next.

It started with one, two, then, in a series of rapid fire pops the bag began to swell. The unmistakable smell and sound of fresh popcorn filled the air. Quong could hardly control his delight as he watched the effect of a microwave oven on a bag of prepackaged popcorn.

With a bag of salted fresh popcorn in one hand and a Coke in the other, Quong was prepared to meet his interrogators anew.

Lieutenant Colonel Jensen was walking down the long hallway to the snack bar when he ran into the two men. "The General is here now. He wants to meet Quong and talk to him prior to making a decision about going on leave."

The three men walked quickly down the hallway to the

conference room they had occupied since Quong's arrival. Captain Smith and General Burkhalter were already inside and seated at the table when the others entered.

Immediately upon seeing Quong, Burkhalter stood and prepared to greet his valuable and important visitor.

"Quong, this is Major General Burkhalter. He's the chief of this operation." As Smith made the introduction, Burkhalter moved from his place at the table to meet Quong halfway as he entered the room.

Burkhalter, who stood almost six three, looked like a giant next to Quong. One had only to see Burkhalter in his uniform to understand why this man was a general. The tall, grey-haired man stood ramrod straight. When in uniform, he stood tall in more than height. Upon his chest he had more than twenty individual ribbons denoting service and bravery as far back as WWII. The Combat Infantryman's Badge with star was evidence of front-line combat in two wars. His sterling silver master parachute wings had been well polished over the years, but they still showed the two small bronze stars denoting combat jumps. If one were to ask—and the few who did usually were ignored—what was the most important item or piece of personal history on the General's uniform, the answer would be twofold.

First, sitting atop the many rows of ribbons, on a single row of its own, was the deep blue ribbon of the Distinguished Service Cross. The nation's second highest decoration had been awarded him during the last days of WWII in Europe. It was there he also earned the right to wear a red arrowhead patch with USA and Canada printed in white. He was one of the last three men still on active duty authorized to wear the patch of the First Special Service Force, the forerunner of today's Army Special Forces, as a combat patch on the right shoulder.

As the two men met—Quong, the small almost childlike

Vietnamese, and the American general who towered over him—there was a pause of only a split second before the two shook hands and exchanged greetings. But in that hesitation, unseen by others in the room and quite possibly only subconsciously by the two men, a quick tally of what each stood for and what each could do for the other was made.

"Quong, Captain Smith has filled me in on what you've been telling them today." Burkhalter returned to his seat and motioned for Quong and the others to do likewise. "I'd like to go back over a few details with you. I know you've been through quite a lot since you left Vietnam, so if you feel we're pushing you just say so. We'll back off and let you rest." Burkhalter allowed his voice to drop as he talked so his final words seemed to almost trail off into a half whisper. It was as if they were the only two in the room at that time.

"As long as I am able, I will tell you what I know. I do not wish to sleep at this time. Perhaps in a few hours I will not be awake, but now I will talk to you." Once again Quong settled himself into his chair, ready for a second round of questions.

He did not have long to wait.

"Quong, I'm going to be very candid with you. I believe what you've told Captain Smith and his men is the truth. We have access to a limited amount of documents that substantiate your employment with us in Saigon." Burkhalter stood and began to move as he talked. He walked the length of the room, sliding his left hand across the backs of the five chairs on each side of the table as he passed each one.

When he was at the far end of the table, he turned and faced Quong. "I'm afraid what you've told us is simply not enough. We, unfortunately, have no way of verifying what you've been doing for the last few years or that any of what you've told us is---"

"Do you think I risk my life to leave Vietnam, to come here and leave my family to tell you lies? Maybe some Vietnamese you know when you were in Vietnam are that way. I am not." Quong was now standing at his end of the table. He surprised even himself by his outburst at the General. Never in his relationship with the Americans had he raised his now shaking voice at a senior officer. These men did not believe him! He was not prepared for this so soon. He knew it would be difficult to convince them; however, he did not anticipate having to deal with someone so blunt as Burkhalter within hours of his arrival.

"General, it is as difficult for me to prove I am telling truth as it is for you to know I lie." Quong was beginning to regain some of his composure. He took a deep breath and tried to calm himself. He could not lose face in front of these men. To do so would bring a great disgrace not only to him but to his family as well.

"If I can give proof there are Americans still in Vietnam. If I give you, General Burkhalter, this proof, what do you do? Do you simply thank me or do you pay me? Do I get a medal? What has happened to others from Vietnam who saw Americans? What will happen to me?"

Quong took his seat. The room was in complete silence as the four Americans absorbed the impact of what he had said and the questions needing answers. The three men along the right side of the table turned, almost in unison, to face Burkhalter who was still standing silently at the far end of the room.

"Quong, you appear to be a very smart man. I think you see the position we are being put in." Burkhalter began to talk as he walked back to reclaim his place at the table. "I also think you're not telling us everything you know. I'll be honest with you. I'd like very much to believe you, just as I believed the many very gallant Vietnamese with whom I worked in Vietnam. There is no advantage, I assure you, of giving us bits and pieces of information. In order to evaluate it and act on it we must know everything you know, and we must know it now." The General stopped and looked around the room, first at his three staff officers and then at Quong. He slowly removed his gold-rimmed glasses, and holding them in his right hand, rubbed his closed eyelids with his left hand.

After a long, silent hesitation he spoke to Quong. "Now, do you have anything else you want to tell me?"

For a moment Quong was silent. It was as if he was in a game of poker. It was a game the Americans played very often in Vietnam. In this game, his hand had been called. He must now reveal his hole card or the game was over, and he would not be the only loser.

Quong had a decision to make, and it had to be made with no further hesitation. He knew he must tell all. Quong decided to play by their rules.

"General Burkhalter, I know you for only one hour but I believe you are good with a pure spirit. I think you others are the same. You realize I am not telling all, but you also, I think, know why. I have no place to go here. I do not know anyone. Once I tell you this thing I know, where do I go? What do I do? I will not go back in Malaysia. Even in Vietnam I lived better than there." There was a sound of genuine concern in Quong's voice.

"I assure you that you will not go back to Malaysia," said Burkhalter as he waited for Quong to finish what he had started so many hours earlier that morning.

It was now Quong's turn to pace as he talked to the four men.

"Because of my sister Bea, I am here. It was she who first told me of the Americans. And it was she who gave this.'' He removed the thin piece of leather which had hung around his neck. As he extracted it from his shirt, a gold locket the size of a fifty cent piece came into view.

''When I left Vietnam I knew I might have to give more than my word for you to believe in me. In here,'' Quong removed the locket and held the piece in his hand as he talked, ''I have the proof you will need to know I do not lie.''

Quong lay the locket on the table in front of Burkhalter.

''Now you can believe that I tell only the truth.''

Burkhalter picked up the locket. The locket appeared to have a fine layer of some type of gum or glue holding the two pieces together. ''May I open this? It's a very pretty piece. I don't want to damage it trying to get it open.''

''I do not have a knife, but if you do, you can open it with ease. The gum around it will keep it water tight and keep it sealed for as long as you do not break the seal.''

Tom Dixon slid a small pocket knife down the table to Burkhalter who used it to carefully pry open the gold locket. Neatly placed inside were three negatives which had been trimmed in order to fit into the locket.

Burkhalter held the negatives up to the light to see what they were. In one negative were two Vietnamese. One appeared to be Quong. The other, a man, could be almost anyone; however, a gut instinct told Burkhalter the man's identity would soon be revealed. The second Vietnamese was dressed in shorts, sandals, a dark shirt and the pith helmet worn by North Vietnamese military during the war. He had an AK-47 assault rifle slung casually over his shoulder.

The piece was obviously a recent shot of Quong and his friend. It was the third person in the right rear of the group that caught Burkhalter's eye.

Tall, slender, with light colored hair and a full beard, the third person in this group could quite possibly, even probably, be an American.

Burkhalter slid the locket down the table for Captain Smith and the two others to examine.

"O.K. Quong, let's say this is real. This man is an American. I've got to know all the details. My first question is who took the picture and how did you manage to get it out of Vietnam?"

Prior to Quong answering, Burkhalter motioned to Smith. "Before you answer, I think we need to call an admin break for a while. There are a few things you and I need to do, Smitty." Burkhalter stood and turned to Major Dixon.

"Tom take Quong out to a BOQ on post. Let him catch a few hours sleep. It's 1630 now. Let's say we meet back here at 2100. That's nine p.m. in case you've forgotten, Quong. I think we should all plan to be here for a while tonight."

As the men rose to leave, Burkhalter stopped Quong. "More than you can imagine, I want to believe you. I want you to prove to me we have men still there and I want to prove it to my boss. And then . . . and then, dammit . . . I want to get them out!"

The hours passed quickly. A fingerprint expert was standing by for Quong's return. A photo interpretation team was already working on the negatives, making photos, copies, enlargements, measuring shadows, distances and anything else that would provide answers to the growing list of questions passed by Burkhalter and Smith.

"Smitty, I'd rather go into combat again than make a call to my wife and tell her we're not going on leave for a few more days." Burkhalter was seated behind his desk in his personal office. Around him on the walls was the record of almost thirty-five years of military service. Plaques, awards, certificates, and war trophies covered virtually every square inch of available space.

"My wife has put up with an awful lot from me and the Army, Smitty. I know she'll be disappointed and will raise hell but that's just a cost of doing business. Well hell, I guess I can't put it off any longer."

"I'll leave if you like," chided Smith jokingly. "I know you won't want any witnesses to your conversation."

"Don't give me any ideas. I think I'll just tell her we had a hot action and you screwed it up. I'll just make it your fault."

Dixon and Quong were driven by the General's driver to VIP Quarters on the base.

"We've got time for you to take a nap or whatever you need to do. I'll stay here with you." Dixon spoke to Quong who sat beside him in the rear seat of the sedan.

Quong selected a couch with leather cushions on which to lay for his nap. "I am very tired now, but I do not think I should try to sleep on a soft bed yet. I do not like the soft of it."

After his nap, Quong was shown the shower. For a long while he stood and stared at the glass enclosure.

"Even in Saigon," he said aloud to himself, "I was able to use an American shower only a few times."

As he stepped into the steamy interior, he thought of bathing in rainwater during monsoons, of trying to wash in canals or small streams of running water in Vietnam. This was a luxury he had not anticipated.

Everything was set for Quong's return when he and Major Dixon walked in at a quarter past nine.

"Sorry we're late, sir. I didn't think I would ever get Quong out of the shower. He said he hasn't seen a real shower for over five years."

"That's O.K., Tom. Just bring him back into the conference room after he's been fingerprinted."

Everyone had reclaimed their seats around the table: Burkhalter at the head, Quong on his left and Smith, Jensen and Dixon on the General's right.

"I hope you feel like continuing for a while, Quong." Without waiting for an answer, the General began.

"I think it's time you told us how you managed to get your information and photo negatives of what may be an American. I think we also need to know how you managed to leave Vietnam and retain possession of this locket." As he talked, Burkhalter unconsciously fingered the smooth inlay of curves and decorations on the cover of the locket Quong had given him.

For a long time Quong was silent, as he felt and saw the eyes of the four men who now waited for his answer.

Quong waited as long as he safely could before breaking the silence. Once he started, he knew he would have to quickly relate a journey which had taken over three months, covered almost nine thousand miles and included encounters with corrupt Vietnamese officials, sadistic military personnel, pirates at sea, and the loss of the entire sum of money his sister had managed to save in Saigon.

CHAPTER 6

The wood frame, two-room house in which they lived was a luxury by current Vietnamese standards. It had previously belonged to a lieutenant in the South Vietnamese Army. In 1975, it had been "liberated" and, like most of the buildings throughout the country, was owned by the government. Minh, because of his work at the compound, was allowed to live there.

Bea and Minh now lived as well as could reasonably be expected in Vietnam. Minh's pay as a Ha Si, or private, in the National Army was supplemented by a ration of rice twice per month. Bea's money from her job as a cook was almost nonexistant, but she managed to bring home food occasionally. Being relegated to a position where she was forced to actually steal food was as foreign to her mind as would be a trip to outer space.

Quong's arrival at their house had put an additional strain on their budget. The only good point about his being there was that he visited the central market every day. There he spent time haggling over prices and obtained the best buys for the three of them. Sometimes it seemed to Quong that his daily vocabulary consisted of only two words; Nhieu Lam! Nhieu Lam! . . . too much! too much! It was a game to be played between sellers and buyer.

Only the most adept of buyers ever won.

By the third day of his second week, Bea was ready to tell him of her information on the Americans and how he could make the best use of the data.

The kerosene lamp cast a yellow glow onto the low wooden table in the center of the largest of the two rooms in which she and Minh lived. They were seated on small, low slung chairs which could easily be mistaken for those belonging to a child.

"Quong, I know you are not happy in Vietnam. You, as well as I, will never see ourselves, our lives, or our country as it used to be." She hesitated, then in an even quieter tone asked, "Would you be willing to leave An Bac? Perhaps even leave Vietnam?"

Quong's amazement at this question was immediately evident. His face at first was drawn almost into a frown and then broke into a smile as his mind and imagination began to drift. He was pulled back to reality by several questions quickly and neatly eliminated by Bea.

"But, where would I go? What would I do? How will I live?" Quong, from force of habit, spoke in a low tone.

"Tomorrow is a holiday in An Bac. We do not work, but instead we must place flowers upon the graves of the men who died fighting Americans. We will talk as we walk to the graves. It is not wise to talk too much here. The walls of my house are very thin and we cannot trust anyone." Bea got up, signaling an end to the discussion. "Do not worry. I will tell you what you need to know tomorrow." Bea pointed toward the small porch on the house. "Minh will not be home tonight. You may sleep in his hammock if you like."

The first time Quong had tried to sleep in a hammock he found the contraption to be both simple and confusing. After several futile attempts he finally mastered the art of mounting the fishnet-like swinging bed. Once inside, he was afraid to move for fear he would be ejected and have to begin his reentry process again.

As he lay in the low-slung bed which he had mastered so long ago, his thoughts began to move to his earlier conversation with Bea.

His little sister, whom he loved so much, and who, by right of his family position of eldest son, was his responsibility, had changed so much in the last few years. Her time in Saigon had altered her to the point where she found life in post-war Vietnam difficult to the extent of being almost impossible. Others, including Quong, had managed to be slowly and reluctantly assimilated back into daily life in Vietnam. Bea could not or did not want to do so. It was obvious to Quong. His only hope was that it was not so visible to others. If so, it could mean real trouble for her. "I'll have to talk to her," he said half aloud as he fell asleep.

Their house was near one of the main highways running north to south in Vietnam. It began well above the DMZ and ended south of An Bac Province in the Mekong Delta. It was the nearly destroyed, bomb pock-marked gravel remnants of this once vital line that Quong and Bea walked on as they went to the Graves of Heroes, as the local cemetery was now called.

After the war, formal religion was outlawed throughout the country. For a nation that had practiced Buddhism since Buddha himself walked the earth, it was a custom the people continued even though it meant they defied the authorities. As Bea and Quong walked among the graves it was not too difficult to determine who here planned for this place in the afterlife.

When a Buddhist is buried, his first objective is to get a gravesite as high as possible. In the Delta with its flat land, only those whose families could afford a crypt or mound above ground got a head start on his contemporaries on their trip to Buddha's open arms. In the northern provinces the village elders and heirarchy were buried as near as possible to the top of a local mountain. Others tried to buy a plot of land near the summit.

Since Buddhists believe the spirit leaves the body by way of the head and shoulders, many people demanded they be buried sitting up. This not only gave them an additional foot or two of height but had the spirit headed in the right direction.

Cautiously, Bea made certain there were no others within earshot when she began. "Quong, I have heard this from a friend in Can Tho whose brother did this. He had been able to write to her through friends in Paris."

"How did they leave? Surely the government doesn't allow a person to just leave? Are there planes or boats leaving Saigon?" Out of caution and fear of being overheard, Quong kept his voice low and made an effort to control his obvious excitement.

"Don't be a fool, Quong! Or course there are no boats or planes waiting to take you away. One must escape!"

Escape! This was a word Quong had not used since their leaving Saigon.

"Together we managed to escape the North Vietnamese and leave Saigon. We will plan your escape together, Quong."

"My escape? You will not go with me? I can't leave you here." There was more concern in his voice than even Quong expected.

"No, I will stay here, for a while. But don't despair; I haven't finished telling you my plan. I have thought about only this for three months. Since Kim Mai told me about her brother escaping I have thought of little else."

For the first time since prior to the fall of Saigon, Quong saw a look on his sister's face which said the Bea who had prospered in Saigon had returned. She had hope once again.

"I'm going to tell you something now that may cost us our lives if we are caught. You would be in the most danger. When you leave, I want you to tell the Americans about their POWs here. But," she hesitated as she looked at her older brother, "I want you do do more than tell them. We must prove to them they are here."

"How do we prove it. We can't take one with us. I know the Americans. They will want more than my word." Even with the inherent danger, both knew Quong had already made up his mind. He would try to escape.

At the small cemetery, few people spoke to each other. There was still an air of distrust that everyone felt. You could not be sure of your friends or enemies these days.

The one young man who did speak to Bea was a soldier from the compound. When Quong was introduced to the man as a cousin from Can Tho, it made no impression on the soldier. Bea and Quong placed the paper flowers and decorations they brought on a convenient grave mound containing someone unknown to them, then left to walk home.

As they left the cemetery they purchased a Vietnamese soda from a street vendor. A small clear plastic bag was partially filled with a flat sweet liquid tasting like a soda but made with tap, rather than carbonated, water. The top was securely tied with a piece of string and had a small straw inserted in it.

They both sipped the warm liquid as they walked.

"One of the things Minh loves most is a camera he took when he looted a shop in Vinh Long. He still has it and we are able on occasion to buy film on the black market. One of the things left intact when Vu Boi fell was a place where photos can be made from film. I know the officer who is in charge. I have seen him many times eating at the compound."

Two bicycles clattered and rattled as the riders made their way down the road going back to Vu Boi, leaving a choking trail of dust as they passed Bea and Quong.

The dust swirled around them, coating Bea's ao dai outfit with a fine thin layer. In earlier times she would have immediately taken the outfit to a woman to be washed and ironed. Now she hardly noticed the stain the dust made.

Quong made a half-hearted effort to brush the dust away from Bea. "Why can't they be more careful. They have no respect for others." He spoke in the direction of the disappearing cyclist.

As they approached the outskirts of one of the small hamlets making up the residential fringe areas of Vu Boi, Quong spoke to Bea.

"How did you, or rather, why did you come up with a plan to notify Americans of their POWs in An Bac?"

Many of the houses they passed were flying small cotton flags with the colors of the Viet Cong or the red flag with yellow star of the North Vietnamese. Most of those same houses had previously flown South Vietnamese flags from the very same flag staffs years earlier. Many would say this was but a fortune of war. Quong did not see it that way.

"Will it ever change, Bea? Will we ever again see our people not living in fear of their neighbor? Can Vietnam ever return to what you and I knew? Am I foolish to even think of such things?" Quong stopped and looked at Bea as he talked.

Bea took a chance on drawing attention to the two of them as she took her brother's hand in hers as they walked, thus violating a custom of men and women never touching in public.

"One day per week, Minh guards an American who is always kept by himself. On days when the American is able, he is forced to do labor outside. The next time this happens we will visit Minh and tell him I want a picture of the three of us." The excitement was beginning to show in Bea's voice. "I will position us in such a way that the American will also be in the picture. This picture will be your proof. It will be enough to bring the Americans back to get their men and me. We are now too close to Vu Boi to continue this conversation," said Bea as she changed the subject to talk about buying prawns for tomorrow's dinner.

Bea and Quong finished their meal of rice and dried fish prior to Minh coming home. The three of them made polite but strained conversation while Minh ate.

"Bea said you were not in the Army during the War of Liberation. It is a pity. It was a grand feeling as we came down from Pleiku. You would have enjoyed watching the puppets of the Americans run like ants. But I'm sure you saw the same thing in Da Lat." As Minh spoke, bits of rice fell from his mouth.

Quong was speechless at what he was hearing. He looked at Bea who shot a look back to him which said, "Please, I can explain."

Minh thought Quong had been loyal to the Viet Cong! What else had Bea told this man with whom she lived?

"Tonight you sleep in hammock." Minh spoke in what could only have been a command rather than a request. It took little imagination on Quong's part to understand why he was being directed to a specific sleeping area tonight. With him on the front porch, Minh would sleep with Bea. Until now he had not even thought about them sleeping together or making love.

For an hour as he lay awake in his hammock, he could hear them talk. It was in low tones and so far away he could only make out an occasional word.

The voices finally subsided and for a few minutes he

thought they had fallen asleep. Minh's groans and heavy labored breathing told him differently. He was listening, in spite of all he could do to distract himself, to his sister and her lover.

Sleep withheld its numbing graces from Quong for many hours into the night.

A silent morning greeted Quong as he and Minh were served fish cakes and tea for their early morning meal. When both finished, Minh went outside to wash. Bea half whispered to Quong, "Minh will guard the American in two days. He has agreed to let me take our picture. Fortunately he only has three more pictures on the film he now has. Once I take ours we will have to try to pay someone to make the film into pictures."

The next two days passed uneventfully for Quong. He went to market each morning, and on the second morning he traded an hour's labor for a cup of sweet black coffee with a half inch of heavy condensed milk in the bottom. Coffee sua, coffee with sweetened cream, was a luxury Quong had not allowed himself since his last trip through Vu Boi enroute to his family home at Ap Binh Tay.

"Today during the midday rest period you must get Minh's camera and bring it to the rear of the compound. I will meet you there. When work begins again in the afternoon we will take the pictures." Bea spoke quietly to her brother as she left for the short walk to the compound.

Quong could hardly conceal his excitement as he met Bea and they walked down the narrow road running between the compound and the airfield. There were few houses remaining on the road. Most had been destroyed during the last-stand battles for the airport when the end of the war came to Vu Boi.

Bea spotted Minh first. He was standing on the edge of the open unfenced land surrounding the airfield. Bea's timing had been almost perfect. Another five minutes and Minh would have crossed the barbed wire surrounding the airfield. Once inside this secure area, even Bea with her ingenuity would have been unable to convince the heavily armed guards to allow her entry.

More important than Minh was the man who walked slowly and cautiously about ten feet ahead of the Vietnamese guard.

Minh came to Wilson's cell after the guard finished his noonday meal. "Wil Son. Today you work. The Liberation Army needs your labor for its good treatment of you."

"Bullshit!" said Wilson, not loud enough for the guard he called Jack to hear. He knew instinctively that Jack was only parroting what he had been told and that he did not believe his labor was required.

"Where do we work today? The canal would be nice." Work on the canals brought two benefits. First, Wilson usually managed to get a bath of sorts after his work detail; and, secondly, he was able to catch a frog or two which he added to his meager diet.

"Today we go to San bay."

The airfield! This would be a day of steady, though not too difficult, labor clearing weeds from around the fuel storage area.

Wilson saw the man and woman approach and immediately hung his head as he was required to do. Most of the time civilians were quickly told to leave when they approached him. This time Jack made no move to impede their approach.

"Stand still, Minh. Let us catch up with you." Before Minh could protest, Bea had moved Quong into position next to Minh and she was focusing the camera. As the two men got into position, Bea shouted instructions to them. When she had them in position, she asked them to stand still; and, in a voice that was half shout, half plea yelled the first word spoken in English that Eddie Wilson had heard from someone other than his captors in seven years.

At the sound, Eddie immediately fine tuned his senses. Had he imagined it? Had the others heard it? Was it a joke, a cruel hoax, or a well-planned signal?

As he watched, the woman jockeyed the two men into a position where they were between Eddie and her. Their backs were towards him. Eddie faced the woman. With a wave of her hand she brought the two men closer and at the instant she raised the camera to position, she spoke again. This time there was no mistaking the voice, the command or the intention. She was speaking to Eddie and he responded instantly.

Three photos were taken of the two men. Minh stood proudly with his Soviet AK-47 rifle slung casually over his shoulder, his NVA pith helmet slanted over his eyes in a pose mimicked since the first time the soldier had seen a camera. Quong talked to Minh as the two men posed for Bea.

"I will be leaving in a few days to return to Ap Binh Tay." Quong spoke loudly as he tried to distract Minh so he would not hear or comprehend what Bea was saying to them. "Bea wants me to take a picture of you back to our village to show our father." Quong knew instinctively that he would get a positive reaction from Minh when he mentioned showing the photo to Bea's father.

The two of them moved as Bea orchestrated their locations in order to get the American in the background of the photos.

Minh finally told Bea that she had taken enough of his time. "I've got to get back to the airfield with Wil Son. He has work to do." This was the first time either of them had heard Minh refer to the American by name.

Quong watched as Minh made the American walk slightly ahead of him as they crossed through the gate leading to the airfield.

"How much more time will we need before I can leave with the pictures?" Quong spoke to his sister as they walked back to the compound. Quong had taken the camera from Bea and had it fastened securely by its strap around his shoulder.

"I will try to get the film made into pictures by morning. The officer I told you about will eat at the compound tonight. I will ask him at that time to help me."

There were no civilians walking or working in the vicinity as they walked, so there was little need for hushed voices.

The remnants of the few houses or shacks which had been built along this main road from town to the airfield had long since been destroyed. The little houses or hooches, as the Americans called them, had been built of any available material. It was not uncommon to see a structure made entirely of metal squares the size of beer or soda cans which had the top and bottom removed and had been split up the seam. The cans were flattened and nailed into place, giving the appearance of neat rows of shingles. Since most of the dwellings were occupied by girls who were being kept by Americans working at the airfield, it was easy to determine the favorite brand of the previous male occupant.

Now, only a few timbers remained upright, with a scattering of tin squares to give evidence of the area's former life.

Bea and Quong arrived at the entrance to the compound. "Give me the camera. I will let the officer remove the film when he takes it to the place where the photos will be made." Bea spoke firmly to Quong as she held out her hand for the one item that could mark them both for certain death if the pictures were too obvious or fell into the wrong hands when printed.

As Bea turned to walk through the opening in the wall leading to the compound kitchen where she worked, she stopped and, without looking directly at Quong, quietly said, "I will not be home this evening. Tell Minh I am staying with a friend who is about to give birth. That is, if he asks. He probably will not."

Without asking, Quong knew what his sister would have to do in order to get the film developed. Neither of them spoke as she turned and entered the compound.

The usual evening meal for the officers assigned to the compound consisted of rice, a vegetable—usually finely chopped cabbage—and fish or prawns in an extremely hot, peppery sauce prepared by Bea. When the young Cheiu Uy she wanted to see this evening arrived, she would make it a point to serve him herself. She placed an extra portion of prawns in his rice bowl.

The officer aspirant took his place by rank at one of the long wooden tables, once used by the Americans in their mess hall. Since the windows of the old building had no screens on them, it was necessary to eat the evening meal and leave prior to sunset or risk providing a meal for the thick black clouds of mosquitoes which converged on every living person in the Delta.

"Cheiu Uy, may I talk to you when you have finished your meal?" Bea spoke softly and quietly as would be her proper place when addressing an officer.

The young man was both pleased and surprised that this woman who worked in the kitchen wanted to talk to him. This was not the first time the two of them had spoken; however, in the past, conversation had dealt almost exclusively with food and the quality or quantity being served. The only other words they exchanged had been when he was bragging to some of the people at the evening meal about the plush new assignment he was given, Officer in Charge of the only photo lab this far south into the Mekong Delta.

Before answering he lay down his chopsticks and turned to look at Bea.

There was a simple kind of beauty about the woman standing across the table from him. He had noticed it before, and he and another officer had even discussed her one night at dinner.

He guessed her age to be approximately 29. That would make her five years older than he at 24.

Like most of the girls who lived in Vu Boi, Bea had shiny, waist-length, raven-black hair. Her finely featured face was much more detailed upon close examination than when seen from afar. She had high cheekbones, dark eyes and unusually white straight teeth. Her finest feature would have gone unnoticed had she not stopped to talk to Cheiu Uy.

Well concealed beneath the ao dai she wore, Bea had unusually large breasts for a Vietnamese.

"Would you like to talk in here or do you prefer to be alone?" The Cheiu Uy spoke to Bea; however, his eyes did not lift as he spoke.

"It would be better if we were outside. I will leave when you do, so you are not inconvenienced by having to wait for a cook." Bea spoke humbly, as befitting his rank and her position, in an attempt to make sure he recognized the importance she placed on his role.

"I do not mind. I will meet you outside in fifteen minutes." He smiled at her as he granted her request.

Bea hurriedly returned to the open kitchen area where she had hidden Minh's camera. Carefully she extracted the black camera and case from a large metal drum filled with rice. Once it was in her hands she quickly placed it inside the small bag she had brought in several days ago for just this purpose.

He was already outside when she came around the corner of the old white stucco building. Since this would be a one-on-one conversation Bea could be a little more forward.

"Sir, I have a brother who has been visiting me from our home village. He is going to return in two days and I want him to take something home with him. I plan to someday marry a hero of the Army of Liberation. Before we marry I want to let my family, especially my sisters and cousins, see what a handsome man he is."

"During the defeat of the Americans, Minh, the man I plan to marry, was able to obtain a camera. We have taken the photos but have no way of getting them printed."

The two of them walked past the guard. The man saluted and waved them on.

"Sir, I know you are in charge of the place to print photos. I would do anything to make my sister jealous. Anything!"

No further explanation was necessary on Bea's part. She had thrown out the bait and it had been taken.

"This is a very nice camera you have. It belongs to your fiance, you say." He took the camera and examined it as they walked toward the building housing the photo shop.

"I know nothing of cameras, but Minh says it is very good. He learned to operate it in Can Tho."

"These photos, they are important to you?" He stopped and, for the second time, openly admired the woman who had come to him for a favor.

Bea drew herself upright, subtly drawing attention to her figure.

The sun had almost disappeared over the western rim of the delta by the time they reached his compound. The dull orange glow lay flat on the ground as far as the eye could see. Nothing broke the line as the sun disappeared. The delta had no mountains, peaks or ridges to block their view. Under different conditions it would have been a classic lovers' sunset. Tonight, for Bea, it marked the end of one day and allowed for the preparation of yet another. Each day, each sunset, and each sunrise were all the same, all without meaning. Tonight's sunset simply marked the beginning of a business transaction.

"This is my room. As an officer I do not have to share it with another. The photo dark room is over here, behind this wall." As he talked he was showing Bea around his room. It contained a flat sheet of plywood which at one time had held a mattress for the American occupant. Now it was the rack upon which he sometimes slept. In one corner stood a small chest of drawers and a metal wall locker, also reminders of the previous owners. A single light bulb dangled from a cord in the middle of the ceiling. His table had a kerosene lamp, which from its condition saw more service than the light overhead.

"We have electricity here at all times. I've got a generator which I use when I work in the darkroom."

"I'm surprised that you do not share your room with a wife. Are you married?"

Bea walked slowly around the room. She stopped at the end of the flat piece of wood upon which he slept.

"Perhaps a girlfriend? I'm certain any number of women would be quite interested in you." As she spoke she moved closer to him in the now quickly darkening room.

"You could give us some light; that is, if you feel it is necessary to have light."

The young man needed no further encouragement. With swift but crude movements, he removed Bea's ao dai and his uniform.

Even as inexperienced as he was, he knew he was in the presence of a remarkably attractive woman when he saw Bea standing before him in tiny panties and a bra which did not adequately contain her breasts.

Their lovemaking was purely mechanical and without emotion. Bea did her best to encourage him in an effort to satisfy her own needs; however, it was over much too quickly for a woman who was fully experienced and finely tuned from her days in Saigon.

"Will you show me how to make pictures?" Bea asked as they lay together.

As if this was a signal to leave the bed, the man leaped up. "Of course. It's very complicated and you must listen to everything I say, but I will show you."

"Did you realize that I do not even know your name?" Bea said while she watched him slip into a pair of loose fitting blue shorts and a pair of sandals. "My name is Bea. Who are you?"

"I'm Cheiu Uy Lu. Officer aspirant Lu from Chi Key. I don't suppose you know where that is do you?"

"I think it's far to the north."

"It's not too far from Hanoi, the capitol of our reunited country."

Bea got up and put on the western style shirt she found in his wall locker. She left the top two buttons open, giving her an available distraction when the time came.

Lu unloaded the camera and took Bea into the darkroom to remove the film from its spool. He then placed it into the small round plastic canister where chemicals would turn it into a roll of twenty negatives.

As it was processed, Bea asked questions about each step.

Once the negatives were dry and ready for printing, Lu took Bea into yet another room where the printer and enlarger were placed.

Once again, as each negative was placed in the carrier, focused, cropped and printed, each step was explained with great detail by Lu.

Sixteen prints had been made when Bea stopped him.

"I've watched you do the others, let me see if I can do one now." Without waiting for an answer, she stepped up to the enlarger and started sliding the negative around under the lens.

"Help me do this one."

"That's right. Get it centered on the board before you put paper in the carrier." He alternated by first helping her move the film carrier and then placing his hands under her shirt as she stood in front of him.

"The image will be a good picture of you. Maybe I'll just keep this one for myself. Would you mind?"

"I think I would be honored if you did, however, how would I explain the loss of a photo to Minh?"

"We'll just print two of these."

The two copies were printed and placed in the tray of developer.

Bea turned to face Lu in the darkened room. "Why don't you let me try to do a couple on my own. Let's see what a good teacher you are. Why don't you go out to your room and wait for me. There are some other things I want you to teach me when I finish in here."

"You must be very careful. I am responsible for everything in here. I think you are good though, so I will let you."

Quickly Bea lined up the negatives and adjusted them in order to get a series of the three photos, one of Quong alone, one of the American Wil Son and another with the three men.

As the image slowly appeared on the paper, she saw that each negative could be used independently or as a part of a trio; however, any one of the three showed enough detail to identify Minh, Quong and the American.

In addition, each showed enough to get all of them killed.

Bea clipped the three end negatives from the strip and placed them inside the back of the now empty camera.

She placed the three prints back into the developer and allowed the chemical process to turn them black and unidentifiable.

Once this was done, she picked up the camera and returned to Lu.

Bea showed Lu the darkened prints. "I did not do so well in that last lesson. Let's see if I can be a better student out here."

She placed the stack of negatives, the camera and the developed photos into her bag and lay it near the door. She stacked her discarded clothes on top of it.

As Bea climbed into Lu's sleeping area, she breathed a sigh of relief for having had an American boyfriend in Saigon who had taken her to the giant photo craft shop at MACV and given her lessons on developing and printing film.

Bea went from Lu's quarters to work at the compound the next morning.

Minh came in shortly after she arrived. He paid no attention to the fact that she had not been in the house overnight.

Quong thought it best to not mention to Bea that Minh had not asked where she was and if she planned to return.

Bea was the first to speak when the three of them sat down for their evening meal.

"My friend gave birth last night. A new life is now about to begin." Bea was talking in generalities to both of the men; however, the message was clear to Quong. Bea had succeeded in her mission.

Later during the meal, Bea shocked them by announcing Quong would be leaving the next day.

"Since this is our last evening together I think we will walk to the market place. This will give us time to be alone, to talk of our family and our village." Minh gave no indication of displeasure in being excluded.

The nightly propaganda broadcasts could be heard coming from the large loudspeakers in the center of town as they walked.

"I made negatives of the three pictures with the American. Don't forget his name. Minh called him Wil Son. That may help identify him." The few people they passed paid little attention to the man and woman as they made their way to the one remaining coffee shop open in Vu Boi.

As they took seats, Quong could tell his sister was burdened with some very heavy thoughts. He knew she would share them with him.

Bea sipped a glass of iced coffee as she surveyed the tables and occupants close to them. Satisfied that she could talk to Quong, she began.

"When we were in Saigon I know you did not approve of me or what I did, but understand I did the only thing I could do. You had a talent for drawing that you could use to get a job. I used the only talent I had to do the same."

Quong tried to interrupt Bea, to say something, but she would not allow it.

"Do not stop me. I must say this to you now. It may be a long time before I see you again."

"One of the things I did in Saigon was save as much money as I could. I bought gold jewelry with it like many of the girls I knew."

Once again Bea checked for people close enough to hear them.

"I still have several pieces of gold hidden in my house. You can use these to buy your way aboard a ship and escape to America. In one piece, a gold locket, we can place the three negatives which I have trimmed to fit. We can place gum from the xa-da breadfruit trees around the edge of the locket and it will be water tight. If the ship you leave on is a small one and you spend a great deal of time in the open, the negatives will not be destroyed by the saltwater."

"What will you do for money if I take your gold with me?"

"Don't worry about me. If—or when—you convince the Americans of the truth in what we say, I will need very little money. All I will need is to hear the Americans when they arrive."

CHAPTER 7

Quong could not sleep. His mind was too full of questions and concerns. From the time he first lay down under his mosquito net, he knew he must sleep and that he could not sleep.

"The journey I begin tomorrow will take me to . . . to France, to my death." Quong spoke to himself as he lay in the quiet dark. Quong did not feel like a martyr, but the life he was now living was worth risking for a future in America.

Bea and Minh had long since gone to sleep. Quong mumbled to himself as he rolled over, trying to get into a position more conducive to sleep. "I must be the only person in Vu Boi who is not sleeping at this time."

Less than a quarter mile from where Quong tossed in his search for sleep, another man also sought the elusive, sometimes peaceful, nothingness of sleep. Eddie Wilson was trying to logically put together a puzzle for which he had very few pieces.

As was his habit, he talked to himself in the dark quiet of his cell. "I can't believe it. My mind must finally be playing games with me. God knows I've given it plenty of changes. Like now, for instance, how the hell do I rationalize laying here talking to myself about some zip broad with a camera. It sounds crazy even to me."

Eddie raised himself to a sitting position under the mosquito net. He carefully re-tucked the end and sides of the net under the thin straw mat which covered the rack of small round limbs upon which he tried to sleep.

"O.K., Wilson, let's do it one more time." He wrapped his arms around his thin up-drawn knees and bent his head forward. "Think. What exactly did you see and hear?"

Like a man on a witness stand about to testify in his own defense, he gathered his thoughts before he spoke again.

"Today, the . . . ." It suddenly dawned on him he did not know the date. He hadn't been told the date since the Commandant called him in to facetiously wish him a happy Independence Day. That was, he decided, three weeks ago.

"Today, the first of August, at approximately 1400, while enroute to a work detail on the long strip, a Viet National female and another Viet male were playing grab ass with a camera. While they were playing, she looked me dead in the eye and said, very plainly . . . in English . . . to me . . . Smile! Nobody in their right mind in Vietnam says smile! There's nothing to smile about, or for. So why me? Was it for real? Did I hear it because she said it or because I finally blew my cork?"

"No! No, dammit! She said it. Not once, but twice. It was plain and clear and it was to me! She took my picture!"

A lone mosquito found its way inside the net covering Eddie. It buzzed over his head and then landed on his thin left forearm. "You try to drill in me and you're going to hit a dry hole. I hardly have enough blood for me; I damn sure don't have enough to share with you." Wilson raised his hand to smash the unwanted parasite. He stopped in mid-stroke.

"This is your lucky night. I'm going to let you go. You're free to leave." He caught the insect in his two hands, cupped them together and slowly slid them under the corner of the net, letting him go.

"Smile," he said as the mosquito flew off to join the hundreds of others buzzing about his cell.

Both men, Quong and Eddie Wilson, finally drifted into sleep shortly before dawn. Each was finally able to sort through his thoughts enough to allow his brain to shift into neutral.

Bea woke Quong as soon as she got up from her bed with Minh. She quickly and quietly fixed a meal of rice and fish cakes with a pot of hot tea. She prepared enough food so Quong could take some with him. Their meal was served and consumed in silence. It was a silence of respect and understanding as well as a sadness.

"Go quickly, brother. The sooner you leave, the sooner I will be able to join you." As she talked, she placed a small blue velvet bag in Quong's hand.

"In here is the locket with the negatives. Along with it, I have two more chains and three bracelets. All are from Bangkok, and they are almost pure gold. Use them wisely. They are the only way out for you and for me."

"To stay longer will make my departure even more painful." Quong turned to go, but instead stopped in the doorway. "Tell our parents, if you can, that I am trying to, to . . . Tell them we are trying to make them very proud of us. They will understand when we meet once again. Toi thuong Chi."

"I love you also, my brother. I will know when the Americans come. I will be ready. Go. The day is beginning. You are all I have. I must now depend on you."

Tears were falling unashamedly from both of them as Quong backed out into the early Delta sunrise.

Torn between the sadness of departure and the promise of another day's sunrise in his beloved Delta, Quong chose to fix his eyes on the new day. He would not allow himself to look back at Bea as he turned his head slightly to the left to wipe a tear on the back of his hand.

Bea's words echoed in his mind. "You are all I have. I must depend on you." Now, even more than when they left the terror of Saigon, Bea had placed her fate in his hands.

"I will not disappoint you, Bea," he said quietly.

* * *

With any luck, Quong could make it to Saigon in two days. His goal was to spend the first night in Can Tho. From there he would cross the muddy Mekong River and proceed North to Saigon, or Ho Chi Minh City as it was now called.

He would try to get a free ride on one of the few remaining buses still operating. In order to get a ride, all one had to do was hop on the bus when it slowed to pick up or discharge passengers or when it made its way around some of the monstrous craters in the road.

Quong had been walking for just over an hour when the bus approached. As he expected, it was loaded to more than twice its normal capacity with passengers, bicycles and cages containing chickens and ducks. Fortunately, he was on a stretch of road where speed above ten miles per hour was impossible.

He prepared to jump on board as soon as the bus got even with him.

It was not a difficult task to swing on board the old bus. In its earlier days the bus had been a 34 passenger model for the U.S. Army. Now all that remained from its past was a few spots of green paint covering areas which had not been wrecked, dented or otherwise destroyed. The seats had been removed, thus giving it a cavernous appearance on the inside. All windows from the sides and rear had been broken or stolen. Only the driver's seat and the cracked front windshield remained in place.

Quong made the trip to Can Tho sitting on the roof of the bus, sharing its silence with one other man as the bus bounced northward. The two men kept a solid grip on the small tubular steel rails running the length of the rooftop.

It was almost time for curfew when the bus finally stopped in Can Tho. The setting sun was reflected on the muddy Mekong River. Quong stared at it for several minutes before he finally realized why. Each place, each person he saw or passed in Vietnam could represent the last time he would ever see them. This was his last sunset over the Mekong River; and its endless expanse of rice paddies and farmers, living in tiny hamlets and villages, would be a memory. It would no longer be a fact to be experienced, but rather a memory to be recalled.

Dinner was a small fish cake Bea had packed for him. After he ate, Quong had to find a place to sleep where he would be reasonably safe. He had the bag containing the gold Bea had given him secured tightly, high against the inside of his right thigh. The flat jewelry fit into his groin area with little difficulty. He would have to remove his pants in order for it to be seen. A quick pat search by the local military would not reveal its location. Even so, he planned to do little sleeping tonight, or any night, until he was in America.

Quong had two items in his possession which could, and probably would, cost him his life if he were caught with them. Less than one week after Saigon fell in 1975, the new government declared that no citizen could own, buy, sell, or trade in jewelry, precious stones or foreign currency. This made his gold extremely valuable, as well as forbidden by the government. The photo negatives he was carrying were an invitation to an instant and violent death.

Quong and Bea had discussed what he should do when he arrived in Saigon. Neither knew how or where he should go to find a boat bound for America. They could only agree that if he was to make it, he must do so rapidly. To stall would be to risk the loss or discovery of the gold. Without it, there was no plan, no passage, nothing.

Quong spent the first day in Saigon at the old Newport docks. Now instead of the large American ships he had seen years before, Russian transports lay heavy in the water at the docks. As in the past, there were many young women waiting on the dock. "Some things in Vietnam will never change," Quong spoke aloud as he watched the activity on the dock.

"There are many changes here, and many more to come."

Quong was startled by the male voice responding behind him.

"Many people like the changes. Many more, like you, I suspect, do not like what has happened, or what will happen to Vietnam.

The man speaking was older than Quong. From his appearance he was probably employed as a dock worker engaged in hard manual labor. He wore a pair of green pants, a light yellow shirt and leather sandals.

"It is not wise to stand on the dock and contemplate change or make wishes. I am about to get a cup of coffee. Will you have some with me?" He turned to leave before Quong could answer.

He had tried mentally to prepare himself for anything that occurred in Saigon. This morning's activities were happening too fast for even Quong to comprehend.

Without speaking enroute, the two men went to a small dockside restaurant which was little more than several large seagoing packing crates joined together and altered with entrance ways and passages. With the exception of the owners, they were alone.

"I see many people come to the docks. They all seem to be looking toward the open sea. Can you imagine why a person would do this?"

The stranger slowly stirred the thick cream in the bottom of the cup as he waited for a response from Quong.

"Many people are anxious to know where the large ships come from and . . ."

"And where they are going." Quong was interrupted in midsentence.

"Yes, I suppose many do wonder where the ships are going." Quong was beginning to feel the conversation was taking on more meaning than he expected.

"Do you know where these ships go, Mister uh, I do not know your name?"

"I'm Luu Tinh. And you?"

"Quong." One name is sufficient for now, he thought.

"I give you my full name, yet you hold back from me. Is there something else you are not yet prepared to tell me? I am here every day. If by tomorrow your curiosity has been sufficiently increased to wonder where the ships go, perhaps I can point out the big ones going to Russia and Hanoi and then some of the smaller ones going to such places as Hong Kong, Malaysia or Singapore." As he spoke, Luu Tinh's voice did not change one decibel as he made the obvious reference to escape routes.

"If you value your life you will not spend the night near the water. Thieves are as thick as fleas on a monkey in this area. I'll see you tomorrow."

Quong spent the night in an old Buddhist temple not

far from what remained of the old Saigon Zoo. Like so many things in the city built by the French, it was in a state of constant deterioration.

The young monks in their bright saffron robes were accustomed to strangers seeking refuge in the temple. All they asked was that the visitor respected the sanctity of the temple and leave a donation when the visit was over.

Prior to sundown, Quong selected a place near the right corner in the rear of the structure. He placed several small denomination piaster coins in a wooden box near the door when he entered, then made his way toward his evening rest area.

Two other men were sitting quietly in the temple. No attempts to communicate were made by either Quong or the others. Each soon retreated into the dark quietness of the evening.

Just after sundown, a young monk entered the building and, without speaking, gave each of the visitors a tattered mosquito net. In a few hours Quong's first night in Saigon, since he and Bea left, would be over.

Quong walked back to the wharf area the next morning. Prior to leaving the temple, he made a quick check of his money and figured he had enough to feed himself for two more days.

When he arrived at the cafe, Luu Tinh was sitting in a corner of the small room talking to a young man and a female, perhaps the man's wife. Luu Tinh did not acknowledge Quong's entrance; however, he was certain the older man recognized him. After almost thirty minutes, the couple left and Quong was summoned to Luu Tinh's table.

"I have given a great deal of thought to what you said, and I would like to see some of the ships which are leaving for Malaysia or Hong Kong. Since I am all alone, it does not matter which ship you show me." Quong tried to make his interests as clear as necessary without blurting out that he wanted to escape.

"The small ships do not keep the same schedule as these monsters now laying in our harbor. They leave only at night from an area nearby on the Saigon River. I must tell you it is very expensive to see them leave. It will cost you the equivalent of five hundred American dollars. Do you still wish to see them?"

Luu Tinh spoke with almost an air of arrogance. They both knew he had the upper hand.

"I do not have dollars or piasters. I have something better. I will bring you several pieces of gold worth at least five hundred dollars."

"Let me see the pieces. I'll decide how much they are worth."

"Tell me where to meet you, and I will give you the pieces at the proper time." Quong knew he was taking a chance. If the gold was taken from him, he was stuck in Vietnam forever.

"Tonight at eleven thirty, a taxi boat will leave dock number 21 at the north end of the Saigon River. There will be others like you there. Have the gold with you. Come alone and bring nothing except one small bag. Anything else will be taken from you." Luu Tinh leaned back in the chair. "It's a long trip out to where the boats leave. We can't have you cluttering the area with personal goods."

He was playing the game to the hilt. If anyone overheard them, or if Quong was a North Vietnamese official, they would have heard nothing more than two men talking about a taxi boat trip.

Quong went to the river well before the appointed time. Had he waited, he might be detained because of curfew. He had to wait somewhere; at least this way he would be closer to the pick-up point.

His eyes became adjusted to the darkness and, in what he estimated to be two hours, he could see quick movement in the shadows. These must be the others, he thought, as they grew in numbers.

Quong had no way of telling the time since he had no watch. By the time he estimated it was eleven thirty, he could clearly count over twenty people huddled in the shadows. At one point a baby let out the beginning of a cry which was quickly muffled. Slowly Quong left his hiding place.

One by one the others followed Quong's lead and moved quietly to the dock. Several families huddled together with their babies and small children. Most were couples. Only three other people were standing alone like Quong. No one spoke as they waited for their escort to freedom.

Quong was the first to hear the distinct and unforgettable sound of a rifle bolt slamming a round into the firing chamber. This single sound was followed rapidly by several others, until the area seemed to reverberate with the sick metallic sound. Before anyone could move, several men in uniform were surrounding the small group. Each man had a Soviet assault rifle held waist high and ready.

The armed men were the only ones to speak. "Dung lai! Dung lai!" They were telling the people to stop. For a second, Quong felt like laughing. Everyone was frozen to their spots. Not a muscle moved. No eyes blinked. Yet these men were yelling for the group to stop.

Quong's first thought was that he had failed. He had failed not only in his escape attempt; but he had also failed Bea, Wil Son and himself. He was about to die on a smelly wooden dock beside the Saigon River as a failure.

He would never be able to tell Bea he tried. He wanted

to succeed, but so many things had changed since he was in Saigon the last time. He had trusted a stranger. Trust like this was risky at best. This time it would probably prove to be fatal.

Quong's breath was coming in short bursts. His chest began to tighten. He felt his entire body grow stiff as he awaited the fiery hot pieces of metal ripping life from him. Other people had told him that you did not hear the bullet that hit you. The sound was not important. "I do not want to feel a bullet." Quong spoke softly to himself.

Quong's vision began to blur as his eyes tightened. His palms were damp. He found himself opening his mouth and turning his head slightly in order to breathe. Less than thirty seconds passed from the time he heard the first sound of his impending execution until he heard the voice.

Just as Quong was about to offer his final silent prayer to Buddha, he heard a familiar voice.

As the voice got close, Quong saw it came from the man walking freely through the armed camp. He also wore a uniform and carried a pistol as a sidearm.

"It is good to see so many of you wish to take a taxi boat ride tonight. I hope each of you brought our previously agreed upon sum. Do not be alarmed by what you see." Luu Tinh walked among the terrified people as he spoke. "I suppose I owe you some explanation. First, let me formally introduce myself. I am Commander Luu Tinh of the People's Naval forces. I suppose you would be more comfortable with calling it the North Vietnamese Navy. It makes little difference what you call me now." With a wave of his hand, he had two of the armed sailors move everyone into a small group.

"Everyone please relax. I will honor my end of the bargain if you have honored yours. Each of you will now pay your passage and you can board the taxi boat for the trip—for the escorted trip, I might add, since I and my men will be with you, to your boat which will take you away."

Although it was a hot night, Quong was fighting off a series of cold, spine-wrenching spasms.

The men passed among the groups of families and couples picking up the fee and then taking an occasional watch or ring and anything else that caught their fancy. Each third person was ordered to strip for a complete search. The soldiers quickly checked the men. It was the women who provided the most challenge. Each female, regardless of age, was carefully and meticulously searched.

As Quong stood silently watching the action, he realized there were only two people between him and a teenaged girl now undergoing a search. Slowly they finished the group and made their way over to the end of the line where Quong stood.

"Ah, my trusting friend Quong." Luu Tinh stood in front of him as he spoke. "Perhaps you were right not to place your full confidence in me. Now you have no choice. You were going to pay me with gold. I'll take it, now."

Silently, Quong reached into his shirt pocket and removed the small bag Bea had entrusted him with. He got it less than half way out of his pocket when Luu Tinh grabbed it from him. Quickly he pulled the metal chains and bracelet from the bag.

"I think this is worth just under five hundred dollars." He turned to the closest man with a weapon. "I want him to be able to leave. Let's do him a favor and see if he has a little more to make up the difference. Search him!"

Quong was forced to strip naked on the dock as the sailors and the others watched. The sailors checked the small bag he carried and then every inch of Quong's body. His underarms, groin and hair were checked. Throughout the search Quong accepted, in embarrassed silence, everything they did to him.

"Put your clothes back on. Get on the boat with the others." The lightheartedness was now gone from Luu Tinh's voice. "It's getting late. We've got to hurry."

The boats were loaded. Two had refugees like Quong, the other was filled with Luu Tinh and his men who would escort the boat out to the ship waiting off the coast.

Quong hoped the other passengers believed his embarrassment kept him quiet on the dock and during the ride. He did not and would not talk to them, for in his mouth was a small gold locket containing three negatives.

CHAPTER 8

Quong talked nonstop at J.M.I. Headquarters for almost three hours. Interruptions were limited to quick clarification of points. He gave them the dates and location of his and Bea's planning of the escape from Vietnam.

By the time he finished, he was obviously fatigued. The activities had worn him down. To continue would be useless.

Quong told his escape story up to the point where he had identified himself to the World Refugee Organization interviewer in Malaysia. At that point Burkhalter stopped him.

"I don't, in all good conscience, see how we can continue to press you tonight." Burkhalter looked at the silver, stainless-steel Seiko watch on his left wrist. "Perhaps I should say, this morning. It's almost one a.m."

"Tom, you and Karl wait here with Quong. Smittie, let's you and I go in my office for a few minutes. I've got some vacation plans to work on."

With the mention of his vacation, Tom knew the General was hooked. He believed Quong and was going to cancel or change his vacation to do something about it.

Smith closed the door behind them as they entered Burkhalter's office.

"O.K., Smittie, let's hear it. What have we got in the conference room? Who, or what, is Mr. Phong Van Quong?"

"That's a good question, sir. We've been with him all day now. We haven't been able to poke any large holes in his story yet. I will admit I'll feel a lot better if we come up with an M.I.A. named Wilson or something close to that who matches what we have in the negative and who disappeared around An Bac."

Burkhalter handed Smith a clear glass mug with a full color print of an eagle in flight on one side and an army unit patch on the other. "This is the last of the coffee. I don't think I'll make any more."

Burkhalter leaned back in his chair and relaxed for the first time since arriving earlier in the afternoon.

"Smittie, I feel an obligation to get what we have up to the Pentagon. We're in no position to put together a body snatch mission. I think I better catch the next plane to D.C. and talk to the Vice Chief. Schroeder's been in the job less than six months so maybe he's looking for a hot item to work on. If he gets half as excited as I am, he'll have a project that'll keep him humping for quite a while."

Smith stood and moved toward the door.

"See if you can get me on a plane this morning to D.C. Give me a couple of hours first. I need to go home. Maybe they've got something leaving around 0800. While you do that, I'm going to cut the others loose. I think I'll suggest to Dixon that he invite Quong down to his place and squirrel him away in the woods this weekend while I'm gone. He should be safe there. He'll probably sleep for two days."

The three very tired men made a half-hearted effort

to stand when Burkhalter reentered the conference room. With a wave of his hand, he dismissed the formalities.

The General spoke as if Quong alone occupied the room. "Captain Smith is booking me a flight to Washington. Quong, I believe you, but I want you to know what we are up against. First, you may have to tell your story many more times before anything is done. And, unfortunately, nothing may ever be done about it. That's not my decision, I'm afraid. If it were, we would be heading toward Vietnam on that plane instead of Washington, D.C. All I can do is present your story and make my recommendations." He began to pace slowly as he spoke. Never once did he lose eye contact with Quong.

Burkhalter stopped, pulled a chair back from the table and placed his foot on the brown imitation leather covered seat. He leaned forward and, once again, spoke only to Quong.

"Now, what do we do in the meantime?" He turned to Major Dixon. "Tom, I'd like to impose on you and Beth. How about inviting Quong for a nice weekend in the country. For at least until I get back. I'm going to see the new Vice Chief of Staff of the Army, General Schroeder, as soon as I can. He's an ally we must have."

He ran his hand through his short, thinning hair. "Do you think Beth will mind? I've already got one wife upset with me today, so I guess I can take one more hit."

"No problem, sir. As a matter of fact I've been telling Quong about my place for the last few minutes. He just told me he's never ridden a horse, so I guess he'll get a chance to saddle up ol' Smokey this weekend.

"Great, let's say we adjourn until I call sometime tomorrow. Tom, you and Karl need to stay close to the phone. I don't know how long this will take."

The temperature had dropped barely ten degrees from

the blistering heat of the day when Dixon and Quong exited the building.

It was not uncommon for the early morning darkness to be as hot as the midday. Those people who worked during the night got no relief from the heat. They had to be prepared to be as hot, sticky, and miserable as those who worked in the sunlight.

"Do you have car or do you use taxi like in Saigon?"

"No, I'm afraid if I took a taxi to work I would have very little money left for anything else. I live almost thirty miles from here."

As they walked to Dixon's car, several mosquitoes buzzed around the men.

"I never thought you would have these in America. I did not bring my mosquito net from Malaysia; but if you do not have one for me, I will sleep without it. I do not think even they will bother me tonight."

During the drive, the two men made somewhat strained small talk.

"Where were you in Vietnam? How did you learn to speak my language?" Quong asked as they drove South.

"I was an advisor, uh, co van my. You know, Quong, why don't we try a little experiment this weekend? I'll attempt to speak to you in Vietnamese and you respond in English. You got any problems with that?"

"I will be happy to try to speak only English."

"One thing," Dixon added. "Get ready for a lot of hand and arm signals. I'm afraid I've forgotten more than I remember."

Dixon drove from Ft. McCullers to the rural community of New Salem. Once in the area, Quong stared at each farm house they passed.

"In Vietnam, so much land as I see here would be split up for many families. That is not so here?"

"No, here you can have about as much as you can afford. I have a little over ten acres. That's about four hectares, if a hectare in Vietnam is still about two and one half acres."

"You still remember much about my country." Quong turned from looking out the open window to stare intently at his new friend. "I am curious. Why did you learn so much and why do you remember?"

"I don't know, Quong. Sometimes I think going to Vietnam was the most important thing I ever did, or will do, in my life. I wasn't important because I made any great contribution to the war. It's just that it was something I felt I needed to do and I did it. I've never tried to explain it before. Do you understand?"

Before Quong could answer, Dixon eased the car off the paved road onto an old rutted dirt road leading to his house. Even at a slow speed, the car bumped and rattled as it crept down the hard-packed road.

"This looks like many roads in Vietnam. I hope there are no mines in any of the holes." There was an air of seriousness in Quong's voice as he stared into the reflection of the headlights on the road.

The car rumbled across a wooden bridge spanning a small creek.

"At least you have much water. Do you grow rice?" Quong asked.

"No, I only grow a small garden and some hay and corn for my horse. You'll see in a few minutes. We're almost there."

The red brick, ranch-style house appeared as they came around a bend. The front porch light cast a bright yellow glow across the entire front of the house. There was a light on in the master bedroom and also the den. At two a.m., this was very unusual.

Before he could get his key in the door, Beth opened it for the two men. "Is anything wrong?" asked Dixon as they entered.

"I'm not sure. I got a phone call about thirty minutes ago. I think it was General Burkhalter. I'm not exactly sure what we talked about, but I thought he said you were on your way home and you would be bringing someone with you. I was half asleep, so after that I can't remember. You know how I am when I first wake up."

"Beth, this is Phong Van Quong. He just came in from Vietnam. He's going to be staying with us for the weekend."

Beth stood and seemed to realize for the first time that her husband did indeed have a stranger standing on their front door steps at two a.m.

Quong extended his hand in a greeting to the lady standing in front of him in a purple housecoat.

"I'm happy to meet you, Mr. Quong." She turned to face her husband. "Tom, he can sleep in the guest room downstairs. It's all ready."

"Great. I know he's tired."

Dixon led Quong to the stairway going to the basement. "I think you'll find it comfortable."

Once inside the room, Dixon turned to his guest. "In the next few days I'll try to make you as comfortable as I can. If you see something or I ask you to do something you're not sure of, let me know. Like the bed, for instance." Tom sat on the corner of the double bed as he talked. "If it's too soft and you want to sleep on the floor, go ahead. I understand. Believe me, I do."

"Sleep as long as you can. When you get up, I'll show you around. By the way, I don't think you'll need a mosquito net down here."

Dixon smiled to himself as he closed the door to Quong's room.

* * *

Not many people work on Saturdays at the Pentagon. Only a few men and women were visible in the offices and hallways when General Burkhalter arrived. By prior arrangement through Captain Smith and General Schroeder's secretary, the Vice Chief of Staff was waiting when Burkhalter entered his office.

"Good morning, Tom. It's pretty early for you to be out roaming the streets, particularly in this neighborhood. Here, have a seat." Schroeder pointed to a large armchair next to a leather couch upon which he was sitting.

"Can you stand another cup of coffee?" Without waiting for an answer he buzzed the outer office and asked for two cups of black coffee.

When the coffee was delivered and both men were seated comfortably, Schroeder keyed a small light over his outer door which illuminated a panel reading, Meeting In Session Do Not Enter.

"Now, Tom, what's this all about?"

For the next two hours, Burkhalter gave him an almost word-for-word repeat of what Quong told him and the other three officers at J.M.I.

"Finally, I want to show you these." Burkhalter opened his briefcase and removed three large prints of each of the negatives Quong brought with him. "He had the negatives for these secured in a gold locket which he kept in his mouth for most of the trip from Vietnam. The Caucasian in the rear is supposed to be named Wil Son; I guess that's his pronunciation of Wilson or something very close to it. I had a photo team look at the negatives prior to printing. They appear to be all right."

Schroeder studied the photos for several minutes. He turned each one several different ways to see as much of each as he could. All of this was done in silence. Finally he stacked the photos in a pile and looked at his friend. "This is some pretty heavy stuff, Tom. What are you suggesting I do with it?"

Burkhalter sat back in his seat and took his time before answering. "I want you to talk to whomever you feel you need to, and then I want you to call me and say go get Wil Son!"

"Tom, you know even if this is approved, no people from J.M.I. can be involved. That would be much too risky to have anyone from an intelligence section like yours on the ground. A capture could be disastrous."

"O.K., I know; I just want to be involved in the operation that pulls a successful body snatch and brings home an M.I.A."

"I'm scheduled to have dinner with the Chief and Secretary of Defense tonight. I'll get an appointment with them for Monday. I want you to stick around in case I need some backup."

The two men made small talk for five minutes, then Burkhalter left to drive to Ft. Myers, VA., where he would spend the night.

* * *

Quong slept until almost noon. When he first stretched out on the semi-firm mattress, he was certain he would be unable to sleep. His intention was to lie on the bed for a few minutes then spread the sheet on the hard surface of the carpeted floor and sleep there. His plans disappeared when sleep overtook his tired body and erased all thoughts of the unfamiliar structure upon which he lay. Even when he first awoke with a start in the unfamiliar setting, a calming instinct took over and he lay in the soft arms of the twilight between sleep and full consciousness.

Slowly, Quong pulled himself out of bed and slipped

back into the clothes he had been wearing since his arrival.

Overhead, Quong heard movement on the upper floor. With a minimum amount of searching, he found the stairway leading up to the main floor. The stairs opened into the kitchen where scents familiar to Quong mixed with very foreign smells. Dominant among the smells was coffee and fresh bread.

"Chao ong. Manh qioi?" Dixon was sitting at the table in the kitchen when Quong cautiously opened the door and peered around it.

"I'm fine, thank you. And you?" Quong returned the greeting in English. He had not forgotten his agreement on the language.

Beth stood nervously in the kitchen when Quong entered. "Bay gio, Ong moun ang gi?"

Even though she mispronounced some of the words, Quong was moved almost to tears by the act of a woman whom he had met less than twelve hours earlier asking him in his native language what he wanted to eat. It was several seconds before he could answer.

"I will be happy to share any food you wish me to have. I am not choosy."

After a breakfast of scrambled eggs, hot, home-made bread and coffee, Quong and Dixon excused themselves and went outside.

"This appears to be good land. I think you could grow much food here. There are fish in the canal?" Quong pointed to a creek running the length of the fenced pasture beyond the house.

"Yes, there are some small ones in it. If you like, maybe we can go fishing this afternoon."

As they talked, the two men wandered around the back yard, stopping occasionally to touch a fruit tree or examine a vine containing small green muscadines. At each stop, Quong tenderly handled the pieces as if each was more than a plant. It was as if each was a living spirit and by touching it he became closer to it. Tom had seen Montagnards do the same in the Vietnam Central Highlands. The Yards believed each thing on earth had a spirit and treated it accordingly.

Dixon knew one advisor who had almost been shot when he sat on a large rock in the center of a village. The village chief believed his grandmother's spirit was in the rock and the advisor was sitting on her. Only after placing a gift of two coconuts and a chocolate bar from a box of C-rations on the rock for grandmother was he able to make amends.

"You have much land here. How do you till the soil? I'm certain you don't use water buffalos." The farm boy in Quong was beginning to emerge in his questions.

"I've got an old diesel tractor. Come on and I'll show it to you. Have you ever driven a tractor?"

Dixon swung the wooden doors of the old barn open. Inside on the left were three stalls which could be used as holding pens or milking stalls. With only one horse, they saw little use except when Smokey reluctantly got a new pair of shoes.

The barn smelled of bales of hay left over from winter and early spring feeding. The open feed bin in the rear of the old wooden structure gave off the sweet aroma of feed made from oats, corn and molasses. Hanging on nails and draped over rafters were saddles and harnesses which Beth kept well oiled and pliable with a combination of saddle soap and neatsfoot oil. Even in the hottest days of summer, the barn had a protected coolness to which Tom sometimes escaped.

"I got this old tractor from a man who bought it new more than fifteen yars ago. He treated it like a baby." As he talked, he climbed on the old green diesel model and prepared to crank it.

"Stand back. Sometimes she spits and throws a spark or two. I don't usually crank it in the barn but I put it here to work on it last week. Here goes."

As soon as the first puff of diesel smoke broke from the exhaust stack in the center of the engine in front of him, Tom knew he had made a mistake.

Since his return from Vietnam, certain sights, smells and sounds were sure to cause a momentary flash-back. One of the things that did it was the smell of smoke coming from diesel fuel.

Inside the closed quarters of the barn, the smoke took him immediately to a little village northeast of Zion. It was here he and his men loaded in armored personnel carriers for an assault on a platoon of Viet Cong holding an old abandoned French plantation.

The men were loaded inside the steel plated carriers. One man was assigned as the machine gunner and manned the M-60 mounted on a swivel ring on top of the carrier. Tom was in the third of five carriers. His best friend, Lieutenant Lee Baily, was ahead of him in the number two APC. The high-pitched engines whined and the five vehicles began to move.

As usual, Tom and most of the men stood with the top hatch open when they rode. There was less danger from a sniper than from hitting a mine in the road. Buttoned, up, a mine would scramble the men. With the hatch open, they had a chance of being blow out of the APC and surviving.

For the first few miles Tom ate the red dust and breathed the diesel fumes from the vehicles in front of him.

The first track passed through the curve in the dirt road with no problem. The second one was split almost in half by an explosion. Pieces of twisted steel, weapons and men, or what had once been men, flew through the air. The concussion was so strong it tore the dust goggles from Tom's face. The fire blown back by the bomb planted in the road singed the hair on his head and face. He and his men were in the kill zone of a well planned ambush. Tom was hit the first time before he could even get out of the APC.

A well planned, properly executed ambush lasts only a few minutes. This one was no exception. Tom knew the NVA were breaking contact even as his assault team was advancing on their position. Helicopter gun ships could not inflict sufficient damage on the fleeing NVA to halt their rapid pull back.

When the medevacs landed and picked up the dead and wounded, Tom could not find Lee. He had disappeared. Tom would not accept the possibility that he had been completely and totally destroyed in the explosion. Not Lee. He would not let that happen to himself. He must have been blown out of the APC, wounded and then captured by the NVA. The only evidence that gave it any credibility was a tape player belonging to Lee which had been found almost a thousand meters from the ambush site. It still had his favorite Country and Western tape in it. Lee dropped it as a clue. That was his style. He had been captured alive, probably wounded, but alive. His name never appeared on any POW lists; but he was there, and he was probably still there. Maybe, just maybe, Wil Son knows him!

Every time Dixon heard the song "For the Good Times" he thought of Lee. That song was his favorite. He almost drove Tom crazy with it in Vietnam. Now it was different. He heard the song and thought of Lee and Vietnam.

Many times, especially when Tom was sitting at the wheel of the old tractor, he thought of Lee, the ambush, the explosion.

The loud enclosed echo of the backfire from the tractor brought him back to reality.

Tom held the black hard rubber steering wheel in virtually a death grip. White knuckles circled the wheel where he had it in his grasp.

He yelled at Quong over the noise of the engine. "Open the door and I'll take her out."

Once outside, he pulled the tractor to a point next to the barn then climbed down, leaving the machine puffing and smoking.

"Lai day, Quong. I'll show you how to drive this thing. All you've got to do is keep the wheel straight and remember which one of the levers up here is the throttle."

Quong's curiosity was overwhelming. With no additional urging, he traded places with Dixon and was soon feeling quite comfortable with the tractor.

Quong was a quick student and in less than an hour he was slowly making his way along the fence line, the master of the tractor. He was leaning forward over the steering wheel like a boy just learning, or an old lady about to forget, how to drive a car. After several trips up and down the line, Tom called Quong over to a small equipment shed where the two of them attached a large mower deck which Quong used to cut almost an acre of thick green grass.

"You keep that up and I'll give you a job as foreman," Dixon yelled as his now hard-working guest finished the cutting.

Dixon helped Quong unhook the mower deck and park the tractor under a large oak tree next to the barn.

"In Vietnam only a very few people have tractors. Most people have never even seen one. I feel very lucky to have shared yours with you."

Tom was cautious as he made small talk and engaged in general conversation with Quong. How easy it would be to say, "You'll get plenty of practice with the tractor. You and I will continue our friendship and you will stay in the area." This would have been unfair to both men as Dixon had no idea what plans Quong, or anyone else, had for him.

Beth called them in for lunch.

"Quong, I have meat, cheese and bread. You may want a sandwich or just eat them alone. Please make yourself at home. I've got plenty of soda and beer, so help yourself." Beth was trying to make him feel comfortable and not self-conscious.

"You have a very nice home here. Do you share it with anyone? Do you have children?" Quong directed his attention to Beth as they ate lunch.

"No, we have no children and we live here alone. Just the two of us." She took a seat across from him.

The ringing of the pale blue kitchen phone interrupted what Beth wanted to be a longer conversation. She answered it and turned to Tom. "It's for you. It's long distance from Washington."

"Dixon here."

"Tom? General Burkhalter. Is everything O.K. with your guest?" The General's voice came over the handset.

"No problem, sir; he's been cutting grass. We're just eating lunch now." Years in the intelligence business taught him to be cautious when using an unsecure telephone.

"I just called Smittie with a scramble. There's nothing in it for you right now. If necessary I'll call you back sometime tomorrow. Anything for me?"

"Nothing at this time."

"Okay. I'll talk to you later." The line began to buzz.

In two sentences the General had told Tom that he had called Captain Smith on a voice scrambler with a classified message and that he was spending one more day at the

Pentagon. This probably meant a second, and perhaps higher, briefing was scheduled for later in the day.

Tom rejoined his wife and guest at the table.

"What about us taking Quong into town or over to the shopping mall this afternoon? Do you think he'd like that, Beth?"

"The new College Center Mall would be a great place to take him. And me too!"

"The place we're talking about is like having the entire village market place under one roof, Quong. It's difficult to describe. I guess the best thing is to take you there."

"You know, I was just thinking, Beth. Quong is about the same size as your brother. Harry left a couple shirts and some jeans the last time he was here. Why don't you get them out for Quong." As he spoke, Dixon refilled his glass with a second beer and offered another to Quong.

Beth brought Quong a long-sleeved, western style, light pink shirt and a pair of jeans. Along with them was a pair of leather cowboy boots which were used by Harry when he spent time with them.

"I think the shirt and pants will fit with no problem. The boots may be a little big. You can try two pair of socks."

As Quong gently handled the clothing, he was immediately drawn to the jeans and the leather rectangle just above the right rear pocket.

"In Vietnam these are only on black market. Most are made in China and soon are no good. To find a pair with the leather patch is something unheard of." As he spoke, he rubbed his fingers over the smooth leather patch with the four copper rivets.

Quong dressed in his new wardrobe and waited for his friends to finish dressing so he could see more of the world he had heard about for so long.

Quong insisted that he sit in the back seat of the car as they drove. His seat placement made little difference since he spent almost the entire trip hanging over the back of the front seat as he pointed and asked questions stop the various shops, stores and businesses they passed.

"I know you had movies in Saigon, but I want you to see a screen so big they couldn't find a building for it. They put it out-of-doors. Instead of seats, you drive your car up and sit in it."

Quong watched in awe and fascination as they passed a drive-in-theatre.

"How large the film must be in order to be seen on such a big screen. This I would like to see."

When they arrived at the mall, Quong was immediately impressed by the sheer size of the physical structure. Once inside the cool, air-conditioned building Quong could not control his obvious pleasure with what he saw.

Although reluctant to enter the shops, he freely partook of the sights available through each storefront glass. He stopped to linger at only two of the many stores he passed.

Two small window viewing areas contained a store display of gold jewelry. Rings, necklaces, bracelets and other yellow ornaments were very tastefully placed on black velvet holders shaped like fingers, necks and hands. These were then illuminated with strategically placed overhead spotlights.

As they looked at the gold, Quong spoke to them. "At one time my sister had much gold. Now it is gone. Because of me she has none. Perhaps I can repay her someday." Even Beth picked up the sadness in his voice.

"You will, Quong, I'm sure of it."

They left the jewelry store and were on their way out when they came to a shop specializing in art supplies. The interest in the jewelry shop was for Bea; this stop was obviously for him.

He needed no explanation of what he saw. His talent and position in Saigon had taught him what most of the pieces were.

He picked up a wooden case containing a variety of colored sketch pencils. "This I had in Vietnam. I drew on a pad like this one." He picked up a large pad of artist's sketch paper placed next to the pencil display.

"Quong, I usually pay someone to help me cut grass like you did this morning. I'd like to buy you this for helping me. Would you mind?"

Before he could answer, Dixon picked up the box of pencils and pad and started to walk toward the checkout counter where he paid for the items for Quong. The smile on Quong's face was sufficient to show Dixon the gift was well received and did not offend him.

Saturday evening was spent as a quiet family gathering at home. After a dinner of grilled steaks, which Quong had last eaten at a cookout in Saigon with MACV, fresh corn on the cob from their garden and a churn of homemade vanilla ice cream, the three of them sat on the large redwood deck at the rear of the house.

For a while Quong and Dixon had a limited conversation. As they had previously agreed, Dixon spoke in Vietnamese, Quong in English. It was Quong who stopped and turned to Beth. "I am sorry you have heard only what I say and not our entire talk. I think we should speak in English so you may join us. It would not be polite for me to say nothing to the wife of my friend."

"You're right, Quong. Sorry, Beth. I know you wanted to talk with Quong also. I'll go get all of us another beer."

"I'm curious, Quong. If you don't mind talking stop it, how many of your family members did you leave in Vietnam?" Beth spoke to him nervously, not wishing to ask prying or difficult questions.

"I have only one sister, Bea, in An Bac. Someday I hope to have her join me in your country. My parents are simple people and know nothing of what is beyond their village. They, like our ancestors, will never leave." Quong swept his right hand outward across the land. "You were born here?"

"No, I'm from Dallas, Texas."

"Oh! I have heard of Texas in American movies. Your father, he is a rancher, cowboy?"

Beth laughed at his interest in a Texan, born of western movies exported to Vietnam. "No, he is a school teacher. He teaches American history at a small junior college. It's not as glamorous as a cowboy, but we did have a couple of horses when I lived at home."

"Do you also have a brother near here? Who helps Dixon take care of you?"

"There is no one other than Tom." Beth realized Quong, as protector of Bea, assumed she also had a brother as her protector.

"You are like Bea now. She has no one to take care of her." Quong's hard stare into the outside darkness held both his loneliness for Bea and his lie about her having someone, since he refused to recognize Minh.

After Tom returned, the three of them talked until after midnight, when Quong began to show signs of his still present jet lag and overall condition of being tired. His drinking seven beers in near rapid succession did nothing for his stability, as they too began to take their toll.

"Bay gio chung minh di ngu," said Dixon as he stood up and yawned.

"Yes, I agree. It is time for sleep. What do we do tomorrow?" There was an air of childlike anticipation in Quong's voice as he spoke to Dixon.

"We'll see. Maybe, uh . . . I don't know; we'll think of something."

Dixon helped Quong find his way back to the guest room in the basement. Quong had no hesitation about sleeping on the bed and was overtaken by sleep almost as soon as he undressed and slid under the lightweight cover.

Sunday was spent without leaving the farm. After lunch the three of them were walking along the fence of three-strand barbed wire when Dixon stopped, turned to face the open pasture and let go with an ear-splitting, high, shrill whistle. He waited a few seconds, pursed his lower lip and whistled once again.

Before the echo died in the oak trees along the side fence line, a large black and grey spotted Appaloosa horse cleared the top of the hill in the middle of the pasture.

When the animal saw someone at his usual feeding area, he tossed his head to one side then shook it vigorously. One more whistle from Dixon was the icing for Smokey. Now firmly and finally convinced that Dixon was whistling for him and would give him an apple or another treat for his trouble, the horse raised his head and with black mane flying raced down the hill to the delight of his audience.

Dixon quartered the apple with his pocket knife and spoke to Quong as he fed the pieces to Smokey.

"Would you like to ride him? He's really pretty gentle. I'll saddle him if you like."

In less than ten minutes, Smokey was saddled and mounted. With one hand on the reins and another gripping the saddle horn, Quong coaxed Smokey into the easiest of walks along the well-worn horse path along the inside of the fence.

"Come Smokey. I will not go too fast with you." He gave him an ever-so-gentle nudge with his knees in the ribs. By an almost mutual understanding, neither man nor animal placed unusual demands on the other.

Quong rode for a few minutes then pulled up in front of Beth and Dixon.

"In Vietnam I sometimes went to race track. I have seen many people ride horses, but only in movies have I seen women ride. I would like to see you ride out here." He dismounted awkwardly and gave Beth the reins.

Beth quickly accepted the challenge, mounted Smokey and gave him an unexpected kick to get him started as she rode away.

To Quong's amazement, she rode as well as the cowgirls of his fantasy.

The three of them spent an uneventful evening of small talk; and, at ten, Dixon suggested he and Quong should consider sleep since they would have to rise at five for the beginning of the day.

Dixon and Quong arrived at J.M.I. headquarters a little after seven a.m., Monday. Dixon saw Jensen's and Captain Smith's cars in the parking lot when they arrived. "Looks like some of the troops are already here. This may be another long day. Are you ready for it, Quong?"

"I am ready for whatever they want of me. I only want to convince them that what I say is truth. Tieu Ta, do you believe me?" Quong did not look at Dixon as he spoke.

"It's not me you have to convince. And I don't think it's the men in there, in J.M.I., either. It's the big guns in Washington. We believe you. It's those guys we have to sell your story to."

Dixon showed his I.D. to the guard and obtained a pass for Quong from the military policeman sitting at a desk inside the main entrance.

"You're to see Captain Smith as soon as you get upstairs, sir." The guard handed a note to Dixon. The folded note had only three letters hand printed on it. P.S.M. It was Smith's abbreviation for "please see me."

"Morning, sir. I got your note." Dixon and Quong stood in Smith's office doorway.

"Yeah, come on in. How was your weekend, Quong? Did Major Dixon show you life on a plantation?" He didn't wait for a response.

"The Boss called last night. He'll be in here in about an hour. Jensen's taken a car and driver over to the airport to pick him up now. He wants you and Quong to see him when he gets here."

Dixon spent the hour going through some work he had neglected on Friday, while Quong thumbed through several old copies of news magazines in the office.

The intercom on Dixon's desk buzzed. "The General wants to see you and Mr. Quong in his office." Cathy St. John, the General's secretary, called them to the meeting.

"Right, Cathy. Tell him we're on our way."

Captain Smith and Lieutenant Colonel Jensen were already there and seated at the small conference table when Dixon and Quong arrived.

Burkhalter was the first to speak. "Quong, I've spent the last two days pleading our case in Washington. I won't bore you with details, but I will say I had to talk to a hell of a lot of people." The man was directing his conversation to one person in the room, Quong.

"We found the name and photo of a P.O.W. that very closely resembles your man. He was an advisor and was captured in '69. He was never heard from again. We believe this man and the one in your photo is the same." A very faint smile broke on the General's face.

"For three years we have been training a team at the Special Forces School for just such a mission." Burkhalter stopped and leaned back in his chair to let what he said soak in.

"I have permission to plan a rescue mission. This was

given to us by people who have even more interest in a successful operation than you and I."

"We have almost everything we need, Quong. We lack only one thing."

"What do you need, General?" asked Quong, as he and the others worked to conceal their excitement.

"The thing we lack is a detailed sketch or map of the compound where he is kept. We can't just jump into this one like Son Tay. We're no longer at war. What we need is someone on the ground that we can trust. We need a man at the compound to guide us in."

Dixon's heart dropped as he listened and understood what General Burkhalter was saying.

"What we need . . . What we need Quong . . ." Burkhalter now chose his words very carefully. ". . . is for you to return to An Bac and meet the team on the ground when it gets there. That's the only way we can pull this off. You've got to go back to An Bac!"

CHAPTER 9

For more than six months, Quong had thought of nothing except his successful escape from Vietnam and the possibility of convincing the American military of the presence of at least one POW still remaining in Vietnam. Once his plane from Malaysia touched down on American soil, he had felt his mission was well over half completed and the remainder would be equally as successful. But now! To return! This was something he, in his wildest dreams or weakest moments, had never contemplated.

"General, I do not quite understand. How will I return? I cannot turn around and do away with my escape." Quong spoke softly, almost in a disbelieving whisper.

"Sir, I don't see how we can expect a man who has gone through what Quong has in the last few months to just . . ." Dixon was stopped in mid-sentence with his emotional defense of Quong.

"Major Dixon, I know how you feel. And I share your concern. And Quong's. Believe me, there's no other way. If we had troops on the ground in Vietnam we could detach some of them for an operation. Unfortunately, we don't. It's a package deal, pure and simple. No Quong, no raid!" Burkhalter turned his attention once more to Quong.

The man was sitting in deep thought. It was quite possible he did not hear the exchange between Burkhalter and Dixon. His mind was filled with flowing memories of the dark reddish Mekong River he had left such a short time ago. During his last weeks in Vietnam, each day was spent knowing it would never repeat itself in time, location or situation.

Burkhalter reached out and touched Quong gently on his arm. "Quong, I can only imagine what this is doing to you. I can't tell you what I would do if I was in your place. It's almost unheard of that a military operation like this depends so much on a civilian, but that's the situation we find ourselves in. You're the key to the operation and the possible successful rescue of Captain Edward Wilson and any others who may be there."

After a long silence, Quong spoke to Burkhalter. "I do not know if I can do this. I will not say yes or no until you tell me more. How will I get to Vietnam? What will happen to me if I am captured? Will you also come back for me? Many Vietnamese who worked for the Americans were left in Saigon when the war ended. If you have a successful operation, will the war be over once again? Will I be still left behind?"

Burkhalter, obviously nervous and a little uncomfortable with Quong's candor, stood and began to move around the room as he spoke. "Quong, until I get your decision, there is not much more I can tell you. I will say that we will be able to get you safely back into Vietnam, and we can provide the names of several contacts who will assist you as you make you way back to An Bac. When the mission is completed, you will be on a plane with the rest of the team. Your chances of leaving Vietnam are only as good as those of the rescue team. Our initial plan says you should be in country less than seven days from return to pick up by the team. That's about as detailed as I can get at this time. For your own safety, we don't want you to know too much."

"I would like to talk this over with Major Dixon. I wish to hear how he feels about it. I understand what you say General, but . . . but . . . I would like to talk to Tieu Ta Dixon." Quong had, without noticing it, referred to Dixon by his Vietnamese rank.

"Smittie, I think we can spare Major Dixon for a while. Tom, why don't you and Quong take the remainder of the day and talk this over. Maybe you can answer some of his personal questions."

Quong and Dixon left the room. Burkhalter, Smith and Jensen remained behind as the two departed.

"If we go on the assumption that Quong is legit and will return, we've got less than six weeks to pull the whole thing off. We've got a three-day period where there will be little moon at night. It's at the height of the rice harvest in the Delta, so most of the military will be guarding and monitoring the rice to ensure a proper amount goes North. There's a political holiday on the third day, so many of the people will be tied up in indoctrinational classes." Burkhalter settled back into his chair and assumed the role of J.M.I. commander. The compassionate man who dealt with Quong was transformed once again into the professional soldier.

"The team at Bragg has been alerted for a possible operation. Of course they don't know where, but they'll be able to guess as soon as Quong shows up and starts giving directions. I want everything we've got on this operation classified TOP-SECRET BLUE and secured for transport to Ft. Bragg. I think we better plan on having Dixon go with Quong. The two of them are getting closer by the hour." Burkhalter shuffled the papers in front of him.

As Tom and Quong left the room, Dixon asked, "Are

you hungry yet? We can get something to eat and take it over to the lake. Say, I've got an idea. Beth is at the commissary buying groceries. Let's find her and she can join us."

Without waiting for a response, Dixon steered the silent Quong toward the door leading to the parking lot. Soon they were driving across the base to the even larger parking lot for the commissary.

"So many cars," Quong exclaimed when they pulled in. "I see so many different sizes and shapes. In Vietnam most were old French Citroen. You do not have them here?"

"I'm sure there are a few around someplace." Dixon laughed as he remembered the ugly machine from his days in Vietnam.

When they entered the commissary, Dixon stopped Quong at the front door. "Quong, I'm afraid you'll have to stick close by me. You don't have an I.D. card so I'm going to have to do a fast shuffle to get you in. If they ask you anything, pretend you don't speak English. Let me do the talking."

Seven people stood in line between the woman checking IDs and the two men. When number six had presented her card and had her personal check verified, another woman came up to relieve the checker for lunch. She wore a tag stating her name was Mrs. Hoover; however, she was Oriental and most likely Vietnamese.

"Hi!" Dixon spoke first. "I need to go in quickly and look for my wife. This is her brother and he's living with us. He doesn't have a card yet and he doesn't speak English so I can't leave him here. It won't take long." Dixon closed his wallet holding his green military identification card and started to gently drag a sheepishly smiling Quong with him.

Without looking at Dixon, the woman spoke to Quong

in Vietnamese. It happened so quickly and naturally, Dixon could only understand the first three words she spoke and Quong's reply.

"Are you Vietnamese?"

"Yes."

As they spoke politely, Dixon watched the many shoppers moving through the aisles. "If Beth sees us and comes over, it could really get sticky," said Dixon quietly to himself.

Quong finished his conversation and gently prodded Dixon. "Di."

Dixon responded to the command to go in Vietnamese. When they turned the corner, Quong broke into a smile and began to laugh for the first time since he left Vietnam. It was contagious and Dixon joined him. "What the hell were you two talking about back there?"

"She asked how long I had been in America. I said one week. She also asked if I came through a refugee center. When I told her yes, she said she knew why you did not want to leave me alone. You were afraid I would somehow get word to the rest of your wife's family and they would all come to live with you."

"Don't laugh too hard. That's happened to a couple of guys I know. They didn't realize how close Vietnamese families are." Dixon began to walk and look for Beth.

"There's Beth." Quong spotted her first.

"What are you two doing here?" Beth asked as she pushed the half full metal cart over to them. "Have you already talked Quong into going over to the Mexican restaurant for a long lunch hour?"

"No, We're going to pick up some stuff and go over to the picnic area at Lake Wingate. You want to meet us there? We'll pick up enough for all of us if you do." Her husband's voice gave her the idea that her presence was expected, not requested.

"Give me about ten minutes to check out and I'll meet you there. Will you be at the pavilion?"

"Yeah. We'll start there. Meet you in fifteen minutes. Come on, brother-in-law, let's go get something to eat." Dixon and Quong both laughed at Beth's expense as they shared their private joke.

After Beth arrived, the three of them sat on an old wool Army blanket which Tom kept in the trunk of her car. The blanket had long ago lost its wool scratchiness and now was a soft olive drab groundcover for them.

Armed with lunch, they spread their picnic adjacent to the large lake used for fishing and swimming by the residents of the post. At this time of day, they could talk without fear of being overheard by others at Lake Wingate.

"Do you remember the Vietnamese bread like this?" Quong asked as he examined the thick French roll upon which mounds of turkey and cheese had been placed.

"Oh, yeah, Let me think. Banh mi! That's it. They used to cost us ten P apiece. That was when we got four hundred piaster to the dollar."

"Even on the black market, you can only get about fifty P for a dollar. And even those must be smuggled into country. The rate changes almost daily."

Quong pinched small pieces of his roll and threw them into the water where they were immediately attacked by small fish lurking around the water's edge.

"Not too long ago, I was in a place where men would have considered killing me for the amount of food I now throw to these fish. For a fish as large as the smallest you see here, they would not have hesitated. I would have died." Quong stared into the dark water of the lake. He spoke to no one in particular as he continued to flip small pieces of bread into the water.

"Was that in Saigon, Quong?" Beth asked.

"No. On the boat from Vietnam to Malaysia."

"Was it a long trip?" The gentle sincerity in Beth's voice was the catalyst Quong needed.

"For 27 days we were on the boat. From the night we left Saigon until we were pulled into port in Malaysia, no person knew if we would live or die. We could have died from no food or water or been killed by the pirates who came on board at two different times."

He stopped feeding the fish and turned to look at his new friend's wife. "Some of the women and young girls still breathe, but the pirates killed them on the inside. They will never live again in their minds."

Dixon gave Quong another beer. "If you don't want to talk about it, Quong . . ."

"No, perhaps this is something else I can tell you and your General. This I can also prove. All that is necessary is to contact the camp in Malaysia and ask the people who came on ship called Bac Mi if they will say Quong tells the truth." Once again he spoke to Beth. "Do you know what Bac Mi mean?"

"No, I'm sorry I don't."

"It means little flower. On a boat called little flower, mothers watched their babies cry until they were too weak to make sounds. Then they died. Others were forced to be witness to the pirates as they raped their daughters and wives. I saw one man have his arms cut off and he was thrown into the water with sharks. This was his punishment for killing one pirate who raped his daughter of fourteen."

Beth began to glance nervously at her husband. Dixon placed a hand on hers to reassure her, as Quong continued.

"There were over seventy of us on board. We had little food and water. Everyone tried to fish for food. Very few shared with anyone else. Even families began to fight over the half kilo of rice we sometimes had. By the time we were spotted by the Malaysian authorities, we were almost animals. War could not do in ten years what one month at sea with no food or water did to the people of Vietnam."

Quong stood and walked away from Tom and from Beth who was now wiping tears from her eyes.

He stopped and turned to face them again. "We were lucky ones. Some ships came in after several months at sea with stories of the people actually eating their dead!"

The look of terror on his face was reflected by one of shock and compassion for his ordeal, by the man and woman sitting silently at the water's edge.

For a long quiet time, Dixon and his wife sat silently listening to Quong. This conversation with Quong brought out a side of the war in Vietnam which Dixon had never discussed with his wife, the total inhumanity of one human being towards another.

"Perhaps you should leave us now." Dixon stood and helped his wife to her feet.

An emotionally shaken Beth walked over to Quong. "Thank you for allowing us to share some of the pain you have had. I will never know what you have been through, but I know more today than ever before how much what I have is worth." She put her arms around the man and hugged him. "Thank you, my friend."

Quong awkwardly returned the show of affection.

Both men watched as Beth made her way up the slight grassy incline and got into the car for the drive home.

Quong was the first to break the silence. "I value our short friendship and your opinion, Tieu Ta. What should I now do? To agree to return will show everyone I do not lie; however, I do not know if I wish to risk my life once again to prove my honor. I am also concerned that without me the man Wil Son will spend the remainder of his life as a POW."

"I think it's a trade off, Quong. If the raid is successful, and I believe it can be with the proper planning, you can place yourself in an excellent bargaining position for a new life in America. A good job, maybe some cash, who knows what it may be worth. Failure means . . . I guess you know best of all what that means."

Quong sat silently for a minute, then spoke without looking at Dixon. "I want you to tell your General I will go if he will do some things for me. First I want to bring Bea back with the team. Second, I will need a job for me and for Bea if she wants one, and last I will only go if the entire plan is explained to you and you tell me it can be done. I will wait until the last possible day for the third condition. The others must be decided now." As he finished, he threw the remainder of his roll into the water. It was quickly consumed by a large fish which had been attracted to all the activity.

* * *

The small, four-passenger aircraft landed at Pope Air Force Base adjacent to Fort Bragg. Since Burkhalter's acceptance of Quong's counter-offer two days earlier, the decision was made to keep him as close to the military as possible. This meant Quong and Dixon were flown to the area by Army, rather than civilian, aircraft.

As the two men walked down the small steps which unfolded from inside the door when it opened, a young sergeant was waiting for them. He was wearing camouflage fatigues, jungle boots and had a green beret with the flash centered above the left eye.

In order to draw as little attention as possible, Dixon and Quong were dressed in a similar manner. Quong wore no rank on his uniform; and, instead of a unit patch on his left soulder, he wore a tab which identified him as a combat artist. In this, and all peacetime situations, the term "combat" was simply a term referring to where most of his work was accomplished. He would be considered a non-combatant, but would be allowed free access to all training areas when accompanied by Major Dixon.

A short ride took them to the low white stone building housing the nerve center for the best and most famous of the American military elite, the Special Forces.

They entered a long hallway lined on both sides with photos of Special Forces members who were awarded the Congressional Medal of Honor in Vietnam. Under too many of them, in the abbreviated citation, was the word posthumous. Most of the men died in action.

"I would like to read these sometime. You will bring me back here before I, uh we, leave?"

"Yeah, I'll bring you back here. We both may learn something in this hallway."

"Major Dixon?" An unfamiliar voice was addressing him. He turned to see a colonel walking down the hall in his direction.

"I'm Colonel Spahr. I'll take you and Mr. Quong down to General McDonald's office. He's expecting you."

The three men were escorted into the General's office by his aide. After an exchange of introductions, the General explained his position. "In a mission such as this, it's best that not everyone know exactly the same thing. Each man can function in his area with his own piece of the puzzle. To that end, I doubt if the four of us could put the entire picture together. From this point on, you will deal directly with Colonel Spahr. He's in charge of the team which we will use. He knows the urgency of the situation. Let me re-emphasize, Colonel Spahr is in charge. You two are vital to the success of the mission, but you are here in an advisory capacity only. Operational decisions are his. And now, gentlemen, you have work to do."

"We'll get you settled in a room and then get an early start tomorrow morning. Dixon, I believe you were a student here at one time, right?" Spahr directed them from the General's office.

"Right, sir. I did the MATA Course in '70 and the Operations Officers Course in '75."

"Good. At least you know how we operate. I've got you rooms in Hardy Hall. You'll have a vehicle and driver as long as you're here."

"Quong, if there's anything special you need, let me know. We've got a hell of a big Vietnamese community around here, so we should be able to get anything you want including nuoc mam!"

The men, especially Quong, laughed at the reference to the foul smelling, fiery hot fish sauce used by Vietnamese like Americans use catsup.

"Your driver will pick you up at 0500 tomorrow. You can eat with us in the field. You can expect to return sometime after 2000 hours."

"Eight in the evening." Quong spoke half aloud.

"That's right. If I use a term you're not familiar with, let me know." Colonel Spahr shook hands, then left them to settle into their new rooms.

The clock was now running. Each day took them closer to the time Quong would have to make a final decision based on Dixon's evaluation.

CHAPTER 10

The olive-green sedan took Dixon and Quong to a small helicopter landing pad next to the large modern brick hospital at Fort Bragg. Already sitting on the pad, engine throttled back with its blades making a dull popping sound as they cut through the air, was a chopper. A large red cross was painted on the nose and both side doors.

"Colonel Spahr says you two are supposed to get on the bird. They know where to take you. I'll pick ya'll up tonight when you're through." Dixon's driver knew more about what was happening at this time than he did.

Once on board, they waited until the engine reached the proper RPMs for take off; then, like a dog sniffing a rabbit's trail, the chopper lifted its tail, lowered its nose and slid quickly across the open space until it gained sufficient altitude and speed to level its flight.

Seen from two thousand feet in the air, Fort Bragg is a monstrous expanse of land. There are training areas designed to support virtually every piece of miltary equipment or tactical situation. The numerous drop zones are frequently filled with the white silk parachutes of men—and recently women—from the 82nd Aiborne Division making their training jumps.

Its woods, swamps and river marsh areas are used for

training for a different type of mission. Clandestine operations conducted by members of the Army Special Forces are practiced and perfected in these shadowy areas. As they flew, Dixon felt they were going into just such an area this morning. He had already determined the chopper was taking a circuitous route as he felt the slow, lazy turns the ship made.

Colonel Spahr met them when the helicopter finally made a soft insertion on a landing zone marked with a smoke grenade as they circled overhead.

"They're playing the game to the hilt. This is just like Vietnam," Dixon yelled across the chopper's noise to Quong.

The two passengers quickly left the chopper as soon as it touched down. They ran with heads bent, in an effort to keep the dirt and debris out of their eyes.

Spahr stood barely in view at the woodline where they landed. "Major, Quong, come with us." Spahr turned and went back into the woods. Before Dixon could ask who the "us" was, he saw a small patrol of about six men emerge from the woods and begin to fall in behind them as they followed Spahr.

After walking at full speed for thirty minutes, they came to a clearing beside an old dirt road which may have been utilized in its past life as a logging road or tank trail. It had seen no use other than from leather and canvas jungle boots in many years. To the left of the clearing, in the rear, was a small rise covered with hardwoods. Beyond that, a stream ran into a little pond of about three acres in size.

Across the road from where they entered the clearing was an area used as a landing zone for choppers.

The entire clearing was about the size of a football field; but by looking at the area and the few men who were visible as they moved about, it would not be too difficult to imagine more activity, planned, simulated, and completed on this field than in the last five Super Bowls.

Colonel Spahr led Dixon and Quong to his headquarters. A camouflage net was draped overhead and bushes were piled up along the sides to break the outline. From more than twenty feet away, the structure was not identifiable.

"Dixon, I've got my Operations Officer and two Team Leaders at my headquarters. They'll brief you and Quong on what we've got out here." The Colonel spoke to them over his shoulder as he guided them to the tent.

After brief introductions, the visitors settled in for a briefing by Major Price.

"As the Operations and Training Officer, it's my duty to ensure the teams are trained and prepared for any mission to which we may be assigned. Our primary purpose is the rescue of hostages, be they political, military or civilian. We have refined the techniques as best we can; however, each situation is different and we tailor our mission to whatever is needed for that one unique requirement. Our purpose is twofold . . . rescue and return. One is worthless without the other. To ensure success, we have two teams. Each is fully capable of supporting a mission and backing up or replacing the other team at any point during an operation."

As he listened, Dixon had the feeling he was hearing a briefing about a team concept which had been field tested. Who had the team already rescued and where? Those questions would probably never be answered for him.

The captains explained how each team was a basic twenty-four man organization. Each was developed to include communications, weapons, demolitions, tactical, and medical experts. Each member was cross-trained in at least one other area. As each finished, he said, "The team will conduct an operation with only the most up-to-date intelligence."

How much did they know about Quong's return to Vietnam, wondered Dixon.

The men were sitting around a wooden field table in the tent as they talked. Of the men sitting in the tent only Spahr and Dixon had been to Vietnam with the Army. The other men had joined the Army too late for duty there. Even though they had no formal combat experience, the two men briefing Dixon spoke with an air of confidence and knowledge that can be obtained only through a live fire mission. This added to his growing suspicion that the team had been tested in operations elsewhere.

"With a detailed description of the area, we can prepare working models of the place where we will make the insertion. Colonel Spahr says this will be a hostage rescue mission. The Colonel says you will provide us the on-site data we'll need." Major Price spoke to Dixon as matter-of-factly as if he had asked for a match. There was an inordinate amount of confidence in the two men built into the conversation simply because Dixon and Quong had been allowed access to the training site. Outsiders were not allowed information on, or access to, this area without involvement.

"Right. Quong can give you an idea of the physical layout, and he can sketch a large portion of it." Dixon was somewhat pleased to allow Quong to assume an even larger role in the operation.

"When we get back to our room, I will make a drawing of what I know of compound," Quong spoke to the other men.

"That won't be entirely necessary, Quong. To wait, I mean." Colonel Spahr turned to Dixon. "Because of the sensitive nature of this operation and the short lead time, I've had all your personal belongings picked up from your rooms. They'll be out here in my chopper in about two hours. From now on, you'll be staying with us. We've already got a tent set up for you."

* * *

For the next two days, Quong made a series of sketches of everything he knew of the compound, the air field, the areas surrounding the two and everything he could remember from what Bea had told him.

His sister had given him as exact a reference as she could about where Minh said Wilson was kept and where she thought the other Americans might be. Each night after work, she added a small detail to what she had already told Quong. There was an empty room on each side of Wilson. Several Vietnamese were held prisoner down the open corridor from him. The guards on duty inside the compound usually slept, but those on the gate were awake all night.

As he drew the sketches, he reached deep within the corners of his brain to recall the most minute detail in order to add it to the growing list of information he was providing.

"Tieu Ta, how long do we stay here?" Quong asked Tom as they arose two hours before daylight on the fourth day.

"Beats me. It looks like they want as much from you as they can get. How much more do you have to give?"

"I think to go on would make me start to make up things that may not be true. I do not wish to do that." As he spoke, Quong slid his legs over the side of the taut canvas cot and began to dress in the darkness.

"We sleep with them, do the running and exercise every morning with them, and provide them information; and yet they will not allow us to train with them or even know what they do with information I give them." The tension and lack of activity was beginning to show on Quong.

Before Dixon could respond, the tent flap was pulled open and Colonel Spahr stepped inside.

"Quong, Major Dixon. I want you to go with me this morning. My chopper will be here after chow. Now, you guys ready for a little P.T.?"

The morning began with a hard, thirty-minute workout followed by a cross country run of about three miles. The first morning Quong had had no trouble with the exercise; but a little over a mile into the run, Dixon saw he was in trouble.

"Easy, Quong. Don't force yourself. These guys are in better shape than you and I together. Come on, you and I will just follow the last man. We can walk and run and make a decent showing."

It was no coincidence that shortly after they returned, a team medic stopped by their tent.

"Major, we've had a lot of problems out here with them little wild ticks. Ya'll ain't seen any of them on your body, have you?" The man had an accent straight out of a poorly written Southern novel. "Sometimes they can take a bite and you don't even know it. How about ya'll roll up a sleeve and I'll take a pulse rate to see if one of them little suckers done got ya."

Before he left, he did a quick check of the two men's vital signs, checking pulse, temperature, heart beat and blood pressure.

Breakfast was the only hot meal cooked in the field. A small mess tent was erected and gas-fired grills cooked eggs, omelets, pancakes, bacon, sausage and toast. One large pot was bubbling with a thick white pasty mixture which would be known forever as S.O.S. A sign at the end of the line said simply, When you get your food, remember the starving people in China. Screw 'em if they can't take a joke.

Quong made the most of the breakfast meal. He loaded his plate with several fried eggs and toast; and each morning as his system became accustomed to the rich food, he added several pieces of the usually greasy bacon or ham.

"I remember S.O.S. at MACV in Saigon. I could not eat at the compound, but I knew one of the cooks. He brought some to his house one day and I tried to eat it." The face he made as he described it was enough to convince Dixon that Quong was no devotee of S.O.S.

They usually spent their time alone together. Several times Dixon made an attempt to explain the closeness of teams such as these and how he and Quong would not be automatically accepted, but he gave up. He only hoped their exclusion would not be taken as an insult by Quong.

Quong was sipping a cup full of a mixture of half coffee, half milk and sugar, when one of the team sergeants walked to the edge of the clearing and popped a smoke grenade, sending a cloud of green smoke lazily skyward.

"Looks like breakfast is over." Dixon stood and walked over to the large barrel and dumped his paper plate and other leftovers.

The chopper came in low, did a hard left turn and landed about fifty yards from the southern end of the road leading through the camp. Spahr, Dixon, Quong, Major Price and one of the two team leaders climbed aboard the chopper as it sat nervously on the ground.

Once onboard, the right seat pilot handed a headset to Spahr and Dixon. They could monitor the pilots' conversation and talk to each other.

"We'll be in the air about forty-five minutes." Colonel Spahr offered no further explanation as to purpose or destination.

Once in the air for a few minutes, it was obvious they were approaching Pope Air Force Base. Dixon could see the aircraft lined up along the sides of the three hangar areas next to the main runways. The aircraft in which they were riding passed slowly along the Northern edge of the area, in sight but well out of the way of the moderately busy air field operation.

Ten more minutes in the air and they began a slow turn to the right. As they turned, Dixon spotted an abandoned runway and several buildings scattered along one end and both sides of the old, well worn field. Halfway through the turn, Quong pointed to a billow of green smoke from a grenade marking a landing zone at the open end of the runway. The pilots had disconnected Dixon from their intercom, but he knew they were talking to the small team on the ground who had marked a landing zone with smoke.

Once on the ground, it was immediately evident what they were now into. With a slight bit of modification and a little imagination, it would not be too difficult, even for Dixon, to place this locale in An Bac Province! This was the training site. Quong's sketches of the last few days had been utilized to transform an abandoned landing strip into a Vietnamese airfield and POW compound!

"Quong, do you see anything you recognize? You may have to work with us on the distances between the airfield and the compound, but otherwise I think you'll find it to your specifications." Spahr spoke to a speechless Quong.

"It is amazing that you could do this from what I said and what was put on paper. It makes me feel excited and a little . . . uh . . . nugy hiem . . . Tieu Ta?" Quong groped for a word and turned to Dixon for help.

"Dangerous? I think you mean frightened, kinh

khung.'' Dixon acted as interpreter.

As they began to approach the buildings, they saw the quick modification.

A wooden fence had been hastily erected to simulate the one of stone which surrounded the compound which Quong had sketched from so many angles. The fence was made of wood but it was painted a mottled grey with off-white designs to give the appearance of the stones on the actual one.

Quong did not recognize the significance of the small building standing in front of the entrance. It was a near match in size to the actual guardhouse in An Bac. The major difference was that this one was an Army latrine moved to its current position. An outhouse for a guardhouse! The interior of the compound was based on data Bea had given him in An Bac. Even though he had never been in the compound, he felt confident enough to correct minor flaws in placement or distances. This on-site walk-through took the remainder of the day. By sundown, Quong was sure the compound was as accurate as he could get it.

One building had a side removed, and in its place a series of barred doors were placed over the openings of five small cells. A roof hung as an outcropping over the entire length of the building. Wooden stools were placed where Quong indicated the guards sat when assigned to this section of the compound.

As he walked along the building, Quong could almost feel the presence of Bea, Wilson and Minh. In a very short time he would be with Bea and Wilson. With any luck Minh could not say the same. ''I will see to that,'' Quong spoke aloud.

''What did you say, Quong?'' Dixon overheard him.

''Nothing, Tieu Ta. Nothing important.'' He half smiled to himself.

As they walked through the compound, the team leaders and Major Price continued to press Quong for details he may have omitted.

"I know you haven't been in the compound and seen the guards, but do you know what type of weapons they have? We have some Soviet pieces you could look at if you think that would help." Major Price made a note to have the weapons brought out the next day, as he spoke to Quong.

"That will not be necessary. Although I have not been in compound, I have seen the guards on the streets of An Bac. Most carry the AK-47. It is the old type; however, I have seen a few with a different version of it I had not seen before in Saigon.

"That's great. It gives us an idea of their fire-power. How about sidearms? Did you see any pistols?"

Quong was aware of two things about sidearms in Vietnam. Only officers carried them, and they were the most prized of all war trophies. "Major, do you ask because you wish to know if there are officers in the compound, or because you would like a souvenir?" Even Quong laughed at his quick response.

Colonel Spahr's chopper landed and the men climbed aboard for the trip back to the base camp. Dixon yelled to Quong in order to be heard over the roar of the engine. "We'll probably get started on some practice raids in the next day or two. Are you ready?"

"Yes. It is better to do it and finish than to wait." Quong knew to delay would place him that much further from his return to Vietnam and the fulfillment of his promise to Bea.

* * *

Dixon was correct in his estimate of when the action

would begin.

"Dixon. Quong. Let's go! Get your stuff together. We're moving out!" Spahr's voice broke through the early morning darkness to wake Dixon from a sound sleep. "My chopper leaves in ten minutes. Be on it."

A quick glance at his watch indicated it was now a quarter after three, and he and Quong were expected to be up and out in ten minutes.

Pants, shirt, boots and pack harness quickly became a part of the men as they obeyed the instructions. By the allotted time they were seated and belted into the chopper awaiting the pre-dawn lift off.

By four a.m., they were sitting on the far end of the airstrip, surrounded by a vicious looking professional team of men who were about to conduct their first raid on the compound. As the new members of the team, Dixon and Quong quickly blackened their faces, donned black gloves and stocking caps and moved to the front portion of the patrol.

"Quong, this is the point where you will meet us when we do a live fire exercise. You'll be guiding either me or Sergeant First Class Lee. He'll be my back-up and assistant team leader. We figure we can hit the ground about this time of day, but we'll get into that later. Right now, just take us to the compound. Let's go from the airfield to the rear wall where you said the guards usually sleep." Captain Miller was the team leader this morning.

The ease with which he moved surprised even Quong. It was if the action was taking place at the cinema at the MACV Annex where he sometimes went. He was a part of it, yet he felt he was detached and watching it safely from afar as a spectator.

The team moved at Quong's direction to the compound. Once at the fence, Captain Miller touched him on the arm. "From this point on, don't get more than five feet from me. Even in training raids you're not one of us, so you're fair game. You could get hurt. Sometimes we train very hard."

As the men moved in the darkness, Quong was painfully reminded of Luu Tinh and his escape from Saigon.

Captain Miller responded to a signal from the point element already inside, which Quong neither saw or heard; and the two of them, along with Dixon and the remainder of the team, moved into the compound.

Once inside, it took a total of nine minutes to eliminate four guards, capture one more as proof of the raid, free the man in Eddie Wilson's cell, move to the other side of the compound where six more men were placed to simulate the additional POWs, and free them. The return to the airfield was a straight line of less than two thousand meters. This was the roughest part since it was not known if any of the other POWs needed stretchers and would have to be carried.

This morning only two of the additional POWs were stretcher cases, so it was not too difficult to move the raiding party and its new members back across the Northern end of the compound to the airfield for pick-up. The entire operation, on its first practice, took thirty-seven minutes.

At the pick up point, Quong and Dixon boarded Spahr's chopper while the remainder of the men stayed behind for a critique of the raid.

"What did you think, Quong? Was it close enough to simulate the area?" Dixon yelled at Quong, as they avoided talking about the operation over a radio even inside the chopper.

"I think it will do very well for practice. I am concerned about landing and take off from airfield. I do not know how many guards may be there."

"Yeah, that could get a little sticky." Dixon thought

of a flight of choppers landing and taking off. They were not the quietest form of transportation. Perhaps Spahr would have a plan.

Colonel Spahr's driver met Dixon when the chopper landed. "The Colonel said give you this, sir." He handed him a small brown envelope.

The short message inside said, "Meet me at J.F.K. Center G-3, 1700." It was signed by General Burkhalter.

* * *

Dixon and Quong arrived a few minutes prior to the time they were to meet Burkhalter. Dixon used the time to call Beth.

"Hello Babe, remember me?" He called from a pay phone outside the main school building. As he spoke, he had to place his hand over his left ear in order to block out the street noise.

"Keep talking, stranger. Your voice sounds familiar. Maybe it will come back to me." Beth laughed as she and Tom traded friendly barbs. "I got a call from Karl Jensen the day you left. He said you might not be able to call for a day or two."

It took maximum effort, and the knowledge that she would not get an answer, to keep Beth from asking her husband just what he was doing. Sixteen years of military marriage left her with many questions; this would only be added to the list.

"Quong and I are having dinner tonight at The Swamp Fox. I wish you could be here. It would be like old times." The situation would now allow him to tell even his wife where he was; however, his reference to the Swamp Fox and old times told Beth he was at Ft. Bragg. That was enough for now.

"Tieu Ta, the General is here." Quong motioned for

Dixon.

"I've got to go. I'll call back when I can. Jensen can keep you posted. Love you."

The two men hurried in the building and into the office where Burkhalter was waiting.

"Tom, Quong. How's it feel to live in the woods again, Tom?" Burkhalter returned Dixon's salute, shook hands with Quong, and then with Dixon. "I know this is not exactly what you expected when you got here, but things have been happening pretty quickly the last few days."

"As a matter of a fact, I'm enroute back to McCullars from Washington right now. Make yourselves comfortable, have a seat. We may be here a while." He motioned for the men to sit.

The men were discussing how Fort Bragg had changed in the last few years when they heard a moderate knock at the door. "That should be Colonel Spahr. We can get on with business now." Burkhalter was waiting for all the main players to arrive in order to lay out the game plan.

"Colonel Spahr, it's good to see you again." The General stood and greeted the Colonel when he entered.

"Gentlemen, I won't play games with you. This is too important to screw around with. I've sold the rescue mission. It's a go! The operation hangs on two people now: Quong and you, Colonel Spahr. I think it's time you got a little deeper into the operation." Burkhalter got up and walked over to a long metal table. On it he placed his locked briefcase. He quickly opened it and extracted a packet with the unmistakable cover with "Special Intelligence-Blue" printed on it. "Come around here, Al. I want to show you something." For the first time, Burkhalter called Spahr by his first name.

For nearly two hours, the four men studied and examined the maps and recent satellite photos of the compound. After agreeing that it was closely represented by the mock-up established at the air field, the men decided the basic plan they had was workable.

"The Air Force will handle insertion and extraction. I had hoped to keep it an all-Army mission, but they made me an offer we can't refuse."

Quong, Dixon and Spahr were once again seated on a large brown leather couch across from the General.

"I've heard rumors for over a year about a new or modified plane the Air Force has been working on. They call it The Black Watch. It's a short take-off and landing model of a C-130 which is completely soundless and is equipped with anti-radar. They've got five of them ready for use and we're going to get two. Under optimum conditions, it can land, let the team off, circle overhead and land again for extraction without an in-flight refueling. I've been doing most of the talking. Do you guys have any questions I can answer?"

"General, I try not to second guess missions like this but I get this warm fuzzy feeling that we're heading West, Vietnam, maybe Laos or Cambodia. Am I close?" Spahr leaned forward as he spoke. "If I'm premature, just let me know."

"You're very close Al; but I don't want to pinpoint it any closer right now, except to say it is Vietnam. The two most important things for you to know are one, that you have three weeks to get ready, and two, Quong will meet you on the ground upon your arrival in country!"

With a somewhat meeker attitude, the General turned to face Quong. "Quong, I'm sorry. I've gotten a little over excited about this, I suppose. I haven't forgotten our deal. You still can talk it over with Tom. If you're not satisfied, you won't have to return. Why don't you two stay here on post tonight and talk it over. I'd like to have your decision in the morning."

CHAPTER 11

The flight to Paris was made on an Air Force courier plane. It left Pope Air Force Base in North Carolina, made a stop near Washington, D.C. at Andrews Air Force Base, then slid across the Atlantic. Like so many other things which had happened to him in the last few months, this was a trip Quong never anticipated.

He and Dixon had discussed success and failure that night at Bragg when he made his decision to return to Vietnam. One factor which helped him make a decision was their mutual assumption that a mission would be executed even without Quong being there. By being in Vietnam when the team landed, he would do two things. He would give it an added measure of probability of success and, most important to him, he would show Bea he had succeeded in convincing the Americans her plan would work.

His being there would guarantee Bea's return with the team.

The latest piece of the puzzle had Quong arriving in Paris. There he would meet an agent who would explain the next phase of his trip back to Vietnam.

The military plane landed in a feather-light touchdown then rolled to the far end of the smallest of the runways at the Paris airport. This took the U.S. Air Force plane out to the main area of commercial traffic but allowed access to the terminal and customs. Since this was a regular stop on the twice weekly courier flight, it was treated no differently than in the past.

"We can go through here and then down to customs. Just bring your bag with you." The pilot, an Air Force major, led Quong through the side door of the plane and onto the walkway leading to the terminal.

Before leaving Fort Bragg, Quong had been given a military identification card. The card said he was a staff sergeant in the Army. His passport and other necessary paperwork for entry had also been provided by his benefactors at J.M.I.

"Remember Quong, we're going to guide you every step of the way. You got from An Bac to the States on your wits and nerve. We're going to make it a lot easier this time. Each operative will identify himself with the word BRIGHTEYES. That's your signal for a friendly." Burkhalter briefed him at the air field at Ft. Bragg then gave him a small worn folder containing Quong's ID card and a well used passport.

The last five minutes were spent with Major Dixon. The bond between the two friends had grown stronger as the time for departure approached.

"In less than a month you'll be back here. I'll tell Beth to ice down a case of beer for each of us. You're going to have one hell of a war story to tell us." Dixon lowered his voice so that only Quong could hear him. "I don't know how I'm going to do it yet, but when that team lands, you can bet your hat and your ass I'm going to be with it."

"Tieu Ta, do not be foolish. You must think more of Beth. I do not want to be the cause of any pain to her. I will return. Do not worry. We have much more we need to talk about.'' Quong took Dixon's outstretched hand and clasped it in both of his almost childlike hands in a sign of respect and friendship. Without looking back, he walked to the waiting plane.

* * *

Quong saw the Vietnamese couple standing by the customs counter. He didn't pay a great deal of attention to them initially, however when they saw him they began to smile and wave excitedly at him.

As he approached, he could tell they were waiting for him. Quong had never seen either of them before.

''Tran,'' the man spoke first. ''That's my brother Quong I've been telling you about. See how well he looks in his Army uniform. Quong! Hurry and come through customs. We have so much to talk about while you are here on leave.'' The stranger spoke excellent English with a slight French accent. Everyone around them who understood the language assumed he was meeting his brother.

The stranger greeted him in Vietnamese when Quong emerged from the quick custom stamping of his passport.

''I believe you've put on some weight. Your face looks fuller. And your eyes. Such bright eyes you now have!'' He smiled as he spoke.

''Just follow us. I'm Nga Thong. I'll be with you while you are in Paris. This is my sister Tran. She speaks only French and Vietnamese, so we can talk freely in English when necessary.''

''We have a place for you to sleep at our house. We will go there now.''

As the three of them left, no one in the group noticed the two men following them. Although Burkhalter wanted Quong to meet his contact in the large Vietnamese community in Paris, he didn't want him to be too far out of reach of the military in case it became necessary to retrieve him for security or safety reasons.

"We do not have much time so you must do exactly as I say." Nga opened the door to his small apartment. "The first thing you must do is change from your uniform. You are no longer an Army sergeant. You are now Phong Van Quong, a slightly radical artist who has been living in Paris for seven years. As you can see from the newspaper clippings in this scrap book, you have had several successful one man shows of your work in Paris.

Quong thumbed through the scrapbook with four pages of clippings. All were dated within the last three years and mentioned him by name. "How well they have proven my time in Paris. Reading these, even I feel that I have lived here. Is there more?"

"There may very well be more but not from me. I am to give you clothes, your new papers, and put you on a plane tomorrow morning. It is not necessary or wise for either of us to know too much of the other. We are both doing what we feel we must do. I know only that the plane I put you on tomorrow will make stops in Athens, Karachi, New Deli, Bangkok and Saigon. Where you leave the plane and what you do is your business, not mine."

As the two men talked, Tran was busy preparing a light meal of tea and imperial rolls for them. Quong could hardly keep his eyes off the delicate beauty of this woman who had combined the very best Eastern and Western culture and dress to her benefit.

She wore a Western style dress but her face and hair were pure Vietnamese. She had accented her eyes with light eye shadow. Jet black hair fell like a river of dark water to the center of her back. For the first time in many years, Quong felt a stirring of a desire to know a woman which went beyond an immediate urge for sex.

As the three of them ate, the conversation was in Vietnamese. Quong surprised himself by asking very pointed questions of Tran. Was she married? Did she have a boyfriend? What did she do in Paris? How long had she been there? Although she responded to each question and the answers pleased Quong, he could not be certain that, under the circumstances, they were not tailored just for him.

"I think it is time for you to sleep. You may get very little sleep for the next few days. You can sleep here, either on the sofa or on a mat. I will leave that up to you. I will be in my room; Tran sleeps in another bedroom." Nga spoke with authority as he practically ordered Quong to sleep.

The quiet of Paris finally made its way into the room where Quong lay staring at a painting bathed in the shadow light of the moon through a window. As he lay quietly, his mind drifted without direction. He touched briefly on the last week in An Bac with Bea, his time at sea on the escape boat and the last month in the United States. He could only speculate on what the next two weeks held for him.

His thoughts were quickly and quietly shattered by the soft sound of footsteps in the room. The slow, steady placement told him someone was making an effort to be silent and that the person was getting closer to him.

His first instinct was to spring from his bed and confront his stalker; however, as he prepared to make his move, the light from the window caught the person and cast a shadow on the wall. The shadow was short, dressed in a robe or gown, had shoulder length hair, and was female. Not just any female. It was Tran!

Quong shifted slightly on his bed to confront her. When she saw him awake and staring at her, she stood silently for a moment, then quietly she slid her gown to the floor and moved into his bed. No words were spoken. None were needed. Not since his days with the Americans in Saigon had Quong been with a woman like this. For over two hours after they made love, they simply lay holding each other. When he awoke the next morning, she had returned to her room, leaving only a memory.

Dressed in clothes befitting a popular young artist, Quong boarded a commercial airline, ready for the trip to Saigon. Since his ticket and his new political leanings were oriented to a return to his old country, he must remember to call it Ho Chi Minh City.

"Remember your code word for recognition and trust no one who does not use it. That is your only link with us. Farewell, my brother. Perhaps we will meet once again." Nga clasped Quong around the shoulder as brothers would do.

Tran kissed Quong on the cheek and whispered quickly in his ear, "Chao, ahn hung. Goodby my hero."

"Perhaps I can return some day," Quong spoke aloud as he boarded the plane.

It took more than twenty hours to reach Bangkok. During most of that portion of the flight, Quong slept or read some of the magazines Nga had given him. All were Communist or socialist-produced pieces, but just having them added a little more to Quong's story. He left the plane only because at each stop all passengers were directed to waiting areas inside the terminal where their papers were checked and they were offered an opportunity to purchase items of local manufacture and exchange currency.

Nga had given Quong five hundred dollars in francs when he gave him his French passport.

"You will probably need most of this just to get cleared at the airport in Saigon. Use it wisely. Each person with whom you come in contact will have a price. It's up to you to determine what that price is."

From Bangkok to Saigon the plane was less than half full. Most of the passengers were Vietnamese. A few were French and a group spoke a third language Quong guessed to be Russian.

"We are now entering the airspace of the Democratic Peoples Republic of Vietnam. We will land in Ho Chi Minh City in approximately two-and-one-half hours."

Quong could see the land mass that was Vietnam as it became visible on the left side of the plane.

Quong, now more than ever, realized he was on his way back to Vietnam. He had escaped and was returning. How long had it been since he last saw his sister and their country? Six months? Six years? Six lifetimes? Could he escape again? Would he have the opportunity?

Since giving his story and his proof to the Americans, he had had the smallest amount of doubt hidden deep within a darkened corner of his mind. It was a doubt about how much he could trust his new found friends. He had never been promised a way out when Saigon fell, but many of his friends had. Most were left behind when America finally pulled out. He was placing himself in an excellent position to have the same thing happen to him.

For the first time since he had faced the pirates in the open ocean, Quong began to get a feeling in the pit of his stomach that death might be about to call in his marker. As the Ca Mau peninsula passed underneath, Quong weighed the possibilities that the Americans may be about to quietly close yet another door on a Vietnamese National who placed his faith and his life in their hands.

"Dixon will not let that happen." Quong spoke softly to the familiar green squares of his beloved Mekong Delta as it passed below.

Ho Chi Minh City seen from the air is a giant of a city.

The Paris of the Orient is spread over the countryside for miles. The many villages and hamlets making up the metropolis were interspersed with rice paddies, giving evidence of the two differing ways of life coexisting so closely.

The landing at Tan Son Nhut was bumpy due to the condition of the runway. Even with more commercial traffic beginning to link Ho Chi Minh City with the outside world, the new government gave low priority to runway repair.

The plane taxied by several metal quonset huts which housed jet fighters and bombers during the war. The ones still standing had laundry hanging from lines stretched between them. Families now occupied these metal caverns.

Quong forced himself to walk slowly and calmly as he moved from the plane to the large white stone building housing the operations and control section for the airport. His main concern was the sign which pointed the way to the Thuong Chinh nha doan, Customs House. Even without the sign, he could have almost guessed the way because of the many armed military men and women lining the corridors in that direction.

"Why are you here?" the customs agent asked Quong.

"It has been many years since I have been home. I am an artist and I wish to show how my country looks to those who have not seen it. I am very popular in Paris. See for yourself." Quong pulled the scrapbook from his bag and showed the clippings from the Vietnamese newspaper in Paris.

"Did you sell your paintings in Paris?"

"Yes, quite a few. But not for very much. Most were sold to my fellow countrymen. You wouldn't expect me to exploit them, would you?" Quong was preparing for his first cash payment upon returning to Vietnam.

"I'm not interested in how you exploited your friends

in Paris. My concern, and yours too, at this time is that we have no provisions for allowing an artist entry into our country."

"There must be some mistake. I checked in Paris with the officials and they said . . ." He was cut off in midsentence.

"Perhaps you should return to Paris and let them help you."

"No, no. I'm sorry. I'm sure we can work it out here. What do I need to do in order to enter?"

"I will have to change your papers. That may be expensive. Do you have piasters?"

"No, I have only French francs but I am sure you could get many piasters for them if you so desired." Quong began to worry that he might have to pay more than he was prepared to do. "Please, just tell me what it will take. If I have it I will give it to you; if not I will have to return to Paris. I have no friends here nor do I know any way to obtain more money." Quong hoped his firm stand would not push him into a corner where there was no way out.

"For you my artist friend, I will charge only one half of all the money you have with you. Come with me and we will settle the account in my office." The guard pointed to a small room where Quong would soon undergo a complete search.

Inside the room, Quong was forced to empty his bag on a small wooden table and then completely strip. Once the customs agent was convinced he had found all Quong's francs, he quickly counted them into two stacks and took one.

As Quong reached for the remaining pile, his hand was grabbed by the man who now held half his money.

"I said my fee was one half. There are others." He laughed as he took another half of the remaining stack.

"Dress and go quickly artist, before I remember that you were not here during the War of Liberation."

Outside the terminal, the heat began to bring Quong back to reality. He watched the few cars, pedicabs and cycles making the swing through the long circle street in front of the main terminal. Few, if any, even slowed down when they were in the main intersection near the entrance to the old US Army MACV Headquarters.

He was standing looking at the traffic when he felt a hand on his shoulder. He quickly turned and faced a man about his own age. The stranger was dressed in a pair of shorts, made by cutting off, at somewhat uneven angles, a pair of pants too large for his slight frame. A similar, loose fitting shirt, sandals and a brown pith helmet which immediately identified him as a driver for a pedicab were all he wore.

"Do you need a ride, sir? I have a pedicab with a very good motorcycle. I can take you wherever you want to go." As he spoke he picked up Quong's bag and began to almost push him toward his motorized version of a rickshaw.

Before Quong could protest, the driver continued. "It is not good to stand outside in the sun as you do. It may hurt your eyes if you have no glasses. You must be careful. You have such bright eyes! Get in, I will take care of everything." The driver's voice changed from frivolous to serious when he identified himself as Quong's contact.

He drove through moderate traffic to the Ga Dinh section of Ho Chi Minh City. The building they entered was behind a stone and metal fence. The remnants of a large faded sign hung over the entrance. The words Angel's Bar could still be seen. Years earlier this place catered to the needs of the Americans. Quong had to make a concentrated effort to block from his mind the thought that for a short period Bea worked in a place similar to this.

Once inside the villa, Quong was formally introduced

to his contact, Van Le Phan. Several other men and women with whom they came into contact were introduced by first name only.

"We feel free to talk here. That does not mean we can be free. I hope you understand." Phan led Quong outside to a large courtyard. Several small stone statues were sitting around in a garden. This was a peaceful place of solitude and beauty in Ho Chi Minh City.

"You are to stay here only one night and then you must be on your way. I am to tell you that you will see Smokey in eleven days." Phan sipped from a small white ceramic cup of hot tea as he talked.

"Smokey? Oh, oh, yes." For a moment Quong had no idea what Phan was talking about and then he remembered the name of Dixon's horse, Smokey. Somehow Phan was in contact with the Americans! How much more did he know?"

After a long night's sleep, Quong was ready to leave the next morning.

"It's best for you if I take you to the central market area and then you can go in any direction by bus or foot. That way I will not know in which direction you go, in case I should be asked." Phan offered Quong a small fresh loaf of French bread. "We have little else to offer for a morning meal."

"Let me give you some francs. I need to change them on the black market. If you can do it for me I will gladly share with you."

"I'm surprised you got through the airport with any left. You were lucky. I do know where they can be exchanged at a very good rate. I will do that and return." Phan got up to leave and then turned to Quong. "I assure you, I will return. Your money is safe. I am your friend."

* * *

The return to An Bac was almost a reverse process of his last trip. He caught a bus to Can Tho where he spent the night in a small room in the rear of an old tailor shop. He heard a man on the bus mention it as a place where transients sometimes safely spent a night or two. Even though he was taking a chance, it was no worse than sleeping on the streets like he did the last time he was here.

He caught a southbound bus early the next morning. By mid-afternoon the bus pulled into Vu Boi.

As he watched the landscape of the familiar area bounce by, he wondered again why he was here. He had escaped. He had made it. But he gave it all up to return. To get Bea and take her with him would have been reason enough, but now he had an obligation to Wilson and Dixon and the other men coming in. He also wanted to see Minh one more time.

Once he got off the bus he walked slowly through the market, killing time. He was not openly recognized by any of the merchants he had dealt with before. Only once was he stopped, and that was by a young teenage beggar. Quong gave the boy a coin and they went their separate ways.

The red glow of the Delta sunset began to spread its wings when Quong started to walk toward the house where Bea lived. He knew the route by heart. He had walked it almost daily when he was here before, but this time it seemed unusually long. He passed the familiar shops and houses, and even recognized several of the local residents as he approached her house.

He could see the dim yellow glow of a lantern inside the room as he approached. There appeared to be only one shadow moving about the room. "Maybe Bea is alone," he said aloud. "That will make it easier to explain tonight."

From the roadside he could see his sister as she moved about in the room. In less than two weeks, she will be able to see what a wonderful home and large rooms Beth has in which to live and work, Quong thought as he stood silently watching her.

"Bea?" He spoke quietly from the front door. "Are you in there?"

"Quong, what are you . . . ? How did you get back?" Before she could finish the sentence she ran to him and burst into tears.

"Let's go inside." Quong steered his sister to a seat at the table. He was pleased to see only one bowl ready for use. "Is Minh here? Is he coming home tonight?"

"No, he works at the compound all night tonight." Bea was trying desperately to regain her composure, as she stared in disbelief at the man standing in front of her. At best, she had hoped to see her brother again in the United States after a successful rescue mission. But here, back in her house in An Bac was something she never expected.

As Quong stood waiting for Bea to welcome him back into her life, she suddenly turned into a woman whom he had never seen.

With a stroke as quick as that of a mongoose attacking a cobra, Bea's flat open palm sprang forth and slapped Quong across his left cheek. Before the blood could rush to the wound, she balled her usually dainty hands into fists and struck him repeatedly.

"You have failed me! You have taken away the only chance we will ever have to leave." Only the sound of a small radio tuned to the local propaganda station with its constant flow of revolutionary songs muffled her harsh words.

"Do you have any idea what I had to do in Ho Chi Minh City in order to earn what I gave you?"

"But Bea, I . . ."

She cut him off in mid-sentence with another firm slap

to the face.

"Do not try to make an excuse. For five years I heard men make every excuse for failure. Now, must I add my own brother to that list?"

Bea was now sobbing deeply. She was striking blindly at Quong. Most of her blows fell harmlessly on his arms and chest.

"Bea! Bea! Listen to me, please." Quong tried to talk to the almost hysterical woman, who was now beyond control and would surely call attention to them if she continued her attack.

For the first time in his life, Quong slapped his sister.

For seconds, which ticked like an eternity, the two of them stood staring at each other. The only discernible sound in the room was Quong's heavy breathing and a short chop of a sob from Bea. The silence was filled with a chorus from Radio Hanoi singing the virtues of working together to defeat a common enemy as the People's Party spreads joy and love throughout the land.

Quong spoke first.

"Bea," he said softly, as if a louder voice would set her off once again, "I did not fail! I succeeded. I came back. I made it! But I came back. I came back for you!"

Even in her anger she could sense the sincerity in his words.

"Quong, I am sorry. I did not mean . . ."

"We have not time for such talk. We must look forward now and not to the past for even one second. Let us sit down and I will tell you what I can."

"Sit here and share my food," said Bea as she led him to the small table. "I have only rice and cabbage this evening. I wish there was more." Bea placed another bowl and cup on the table. The old glass in the center of the table held several pairs of chopsticks. Quong reached for two and checked to make certain they were the same size.

"I know you have many questions to ask of me and I will answer them as best I can. Perhaps we should wait until the propaganda broadcasts begin. That will give us a little more outside noise to cover our conversation." As Quong spoke, Bea reached across the small wooden table and took his hand in hers, squeezing it like a long lost lover.

For the benefit of the others living in the rest of the house, they talked of local news as they ate dinner.

"The rice fields along the Song Bay river are almost ready for harvest. I saw them as I came up from Ap Binh Tay."

"I have missed your company since you returned to our home village, Quong."

This banter continued until the crackle of loudspeakers warming up for the nightly broadcasts could be heard outside.

"Since you left, the other couple in the house bought their own radio. They will have it turned on, so we can speak more freely." The excitement and anticipation was growing in Bea's voice.

Bea sat, spellbound, as Quong told of his escape through the Saigon docks, at sea, and of the gold locket he kept in his mouth.

"Why was it so hard to convince the Americans to return for their men? Surely they must still be looking for them." Bea had a difficult time trying to understand the politics which Quong had gone through.

"What do we do now? Why did you agree to return?" With a start, Bea asked, wide eyed, "They are coming, aren't they? You did not return to stay. You said . . ."

"Do not worry. There is much I must do, but we will be out of An Bac in a very short time. Before that happens, I will need your help. The plan will not work without you. It will be even more dangerous now than before, but I must ask you to do it."

"After what you have been through, do not worry about me. I will do whatever is necessary to support you."

As Quong prepared for sleep, he thought of how his role had changed. During his last visit, Bea was in control and he did what she asked. Now it was Quong assuming his traditional role of older brother and leader of his sister.

CHAPTER 12

The decision was made. Captain J. D. "Jake" Miller would lead his team in first. His second-in-command was First Lieutenant Guy Nelson. In addition, Nelson would be in charge of the five man security team. He would ensure the assault team got in and out safely. A total of twelve men would be on the ground.

A back-up team of exactly the same size and configuration would circle overhead in the second Black Watch ship. This second team was ready for any eventuality. The team was prepared to take over the mission if something happened to Miller's men on the way in . They could land and secure the airfield for extraction or, in the unlikely event the first team got in over its head, they would fight their way in to relieve them.

During training, both teams rotated through the practice raids. They made endless assault landings, raids and extractions. Early morning, late night and even a few daylight missions were practiced.

Because the practice was done on an active military installation where Special Forces trained, there was no great worry of Soviet satellites picking up the increased activity. With the exception of the actions on the airfield, most of it was done under cover or inside the row of buildings, thus further limiting outside detection.

* * *

The radio crackled. First it was just static and the increasing volume sound of a handset being depressed. The voice tumbled forth in a short tense manner.

"Shiloh. This is Gettysburg, over."

A young private leaned over from the front seat of the jeep and picked up the handset. "Colonel Spahr, it's for you, sir."

"Who is it? Did you get the call sign?"

"Yes, sir. It was Gettysburg."

"Gettysburg. This is Shiloh, over." Spahr responded immediately upon learning the other's call sign.

"Shiloh, I want you to meet me at Appomattox. You'll have to ride your horse in. How long before you can be here?" Major General Burkhalter, Gettysburg on the radio, was telling Spahr to drive into the Special Forces Headquarters.

"Roger. Gettysburg, I'll be there in nine zero minutes, over." Even using the paved roads from the main training area, the drive would take an hour and a half.

"Okay Shiloh. I'm waiting. See you in nine zero. Out." Burkhalter signed off without giving any indication of why he wanted the meeting. Perhaps it was for a progress report. If they followed the current schedule, the team had less than ten days before they moved out.

As they passed the main post exchange and turned into the headquarters area, Spahr's driver turned to him. "How long you think we gonna be up here, sir. I'd like to run over to the P.X. and pick up some new razor blades. I been using the same one for almost two weeks now. I been doing things to my face that I could go to jail for."

"Yeah, okay. Don't be in there too long. I don't know how long this will take." Spahr almost jumped from the jeep before it came to a complete stop. "And stay away from the skin books. We're not going down on Hay Street before I take you back to the woods. I don't care how horny you get." Specialist Tommy Hamilton had been driving for Spahr since the young man was assigned to Group Headquarters. He was fully qualified as a Special Forces radio operator and was the dedicated, energetic soldier Spahr looked for in all his men. Sometimes Spahr even showed him a glimmer of compassion.

As Spahr entered the headquarters, he took a second to bend down and pull his bloused camouflage fatigue pants straight over the tops of his boots. His beret was removed and tucked into the large pocket on the thigh of his right pant leg.

"Over here, Colonel," Sergeant Major Bill Moore motioned for him. "Your man is in here."

The command conference room was a completely secure area. It was checked before and after each briefing carrying classification of Secret or higher. No one was allowed to enter or exit without first leaving their I.D. card with a guard at a table by the door.

Spahr's I.D. card was placed in a locked box by the door guard. After this procedure was routinely accomplished, a buzzer was activated and the door was unlocked, giving Spahr access to the room.

Burkhalter, Dixon and Captain Smith were already seated and waiting for Spahr. "Colonel, I want you to meet my XO, Captain Bill Smith. Bill, this is Colonel Al Spahr. He's the man behind the scenes on the operation."

"Glad to meet you, Captain." Spahr shook hands with the Navy officer.

"My pleasure. Call me Smittie. We may as well get on a first name basis. We're going to be seeing a lot of each other in the near future.''

''Have a seat, Al. I want to bring you up to speed on what's happened to Quong in the last few days. Smittie, you want to give him a copy of the radio traffic?'' Smith slid a copy of a message across the table to Spahr.

''Quong made it back to Ho Chi Minh City. We had him picked up by a Viet national in Paris and by another one in Vietnam. We've heard from both of them that he is in good shape and on time.''

Spahr's face gave away his composure. ''Excuse me, but did you say you heard from a contact in Ho Chi Minh City? Isn't that a little risky? I mean, an operative in Vietnam has got to be worth his weight in gold. How do you know Quong didn't blow his cover?''

''Unfortunately, we don't. It was a calculated risk we had to take. We have to know if he makes it back to An Bac. We should hear one more report before we get a go-ahead.'' Smith, as Naval Intelligence representative, answered Spahr.

''Al, do you remember reading about or seeing some of the old movies about the coast watchers we had in the Pacific in World War II? Well, we've got a smaller but similar program in Vietnam. There are still a few people over there who, for whatever reason, are feeding us info. Some are stationary. Some keep on the move. We manage to get messages in or out with some regularity.''

Burkhalter waited a second for this to be absorbed, then leaned back in his chair. ''Basically what this means, Al, is we have Quong on the ground in the right spot now to lead you in. I want you to intensify the training. Get everything ready and be prepared to lift off in eight days. I'll need a complete troop list of all personnel in three days and a final arms and equipment list in five. From now on, you'll deal directly with Smittie. We've set up a joint exercise between a Navy Seal team and a Special

Forces A team, so that will give Smittie some cover and an excuse to be here. I'll be monitoring everything from J.M.I. Headquarters, up until the time you depart. After that, I'll move my headquarters up to Langley, Virginia. Now, do you or anyone else have any questions?" Burkhalter looked at each man in turn, Spahr, Smith and Dixon.

Dixon was the first to speak. "Sir . . ." he paused for several seconds. His eyes were cast down, and he fumbled almost unconsciously with his wrist watch. "Sir, I want to go. I want to be on the team when it hits the ground. I owe that to Quong. I've given it a great deal of thought and I can fit in with the assault team."

Spahr was the first to speak. "I don't think it would be a good idea. I mean, my team leaders are fully capable of handling the mission. That's what we've trained for. And as you know, sir, although this is the team's first trip to Vietnam, this is not our first body snatch . . ."

"Colonel, I'm not asking to be the team leader." Dixon spoke directly to Spahr. "I've already had a team in combat. All I'm saying is, I know Quong. He's the key piece to the whole pie. You just may need me there. Remember, I speak the language, too. Your team does not have that capability."

The men sat silently, each waiting for the others to speak.

"Tom, I hear you and I understand what you're saying, but I'll leave that decision up to Colonel Spahr. I'm not too excited about having someone from J.M.I. on the ground if it's a wash out, but I'm confident we're going to succeed. Al, it's your call. I, and Tom, will support your decision." Burkhalter spoke in a tone of voice that reinforced what he said.

Spahr looked first at the General, then at Tom. "Major," he said with no hint of animosity, "you've got three days to convince me your name should be on the troop list when I give it to General Burkhalter. You think you can do it?"

"Just give me a chance, sir. I won't disappoint you, here or in Vietnam." Although this was deadly serious, Dixon had to make a concentrated effort not to break into a grin.

The longest, slowest, seventy-two hours of Dixon's life finally passed. For three days he made almost every assault, insertion and extraction with both teams. The men, and even the two team leaders, softened toward him and accepted him as a straphanger who could, and did, carry his own weight. If Colonel Spahr was convinced, Dixon would soon be enroute to Vietnam.

The sun was almost gone as it made its way from the North Carolina sky enroute to its neighbors to the west when the chopper came in low at treetop level. With no flair or formalities it landed on the base camp landing pad. As quickly as it came in, the ship lifted off and left. The only reminder that it had been there was its passenger. Colonel Spahr was walking toward his headquarters tent.

"Okay guys, we're going on a little trip again. Needless to say, from this point on everyone is restricted to the camp. No one leaves and there will be no radio traffic unless I approve it." Spahr began to pace in front of the tent as he talked.

He pointed, in general terms, to the green grass around him and then at his men. "Why don't you all pick a nice comfortable place and sit down. This may take a few minutes."

He produced a lined yellow sheet of paper from his pocket and unfolded it. Every man who had gone through a briefing like this before knew the names of those men going were listed on the paper. Each had heard his name at least once.

"All right," Spahr cleared his throat and began. "Captain Miller, it's your show. Your team is primary; Morgan, you're back-up. Lieutenant Nelson, you're the security team leader. The following NCO's will be on the ground with Miller; Sergeant Lee, you're the XO and in charge of demo. This time Harry, let's don't have any theatrics." The tension and excitement was momentarily put aside as the men remembered SFC Harry Lee's last exploit.

For a firepower demonstration at the J.F.K. School recently, Lee had been required to place charges in five areas. He blew a stump, a tree, a wrecked jeep, a hasty bridge and a bunker. All went without a hitch until he finished and got on the public address system to address the on-lookers, which included several local dignitaries and members of the press.

"Ladies and gentlemen," he began. "What you have just seen is a demonstration by the best demolition man in the best outfit in the United States Army." He proceeded to tell them about Special Forces training in general and his expertise in particular. Never being one to let well enough alone, he ended with, "A good demo man, and I am the best, can set a well-placed charge on a woman and blow her nipples off without making her tits shake!"

Lee had been a member of the team since it had moved from concept to actuality several years earlier. Although he occasionally felt he was required to get drunk and tear up a local Fayetteville bar and a few locals, he could be counted on explicitly when in a training or live mission.

"Lee, you'll have Sergeants Drake, Phillips, Stern and Richards behind you. Sergeant Tiny Holt will handle the assault team."

"And anything else he wants to handle," came from the small group. The quips were a part of each briefing, to break the deadly seriousness of the situation. With luck, each man would return, but there was an inherent possibility that some would not.

"Lieutenant Nelson, you've got Sergeants Waterson, Tomczak and Chan. Doc Scott will be the medic. Morgan, your team will back them up."

Spahr gave the troop list to Major Price.

Dixon was nervously aware that his name had not been called.

"Now, one other thing." Although he spoke to his men, he was looking straight at Dixon. "I'm going to add one man to the team. He's not in the chain of command. Miller, you're still in absolute, complete control. Let's just say he's a liaison between us and friendly civilians."

Dixon's smile gave away his feelings.

He knew how he would feel in a similar situation; however, he also knew Quong was waiting in An Bac for a group of men in whom he was still reluctant to place his entire trust. After all, he had been left in Saigon. Maybe with me there, he'll feel better about these guys. Dixon almost spoke his thoughts aloud.

"Now for the biggie. Is anyone concerned about where we're going?"

Before Spahr could answer his own question, the general mood of the team was summed up by Sergeant Tiny Holt when he responded, "Who gives a shit, sir. Just point us in the right direction. Let's pull pitch and go."

The bravado Dixon noticed during the training carried through now that they were getting a mission. It was sincere and honest and not, as he suspected at times, simply a power play.

Spahr was now leaning with his back resting against one of the large tall pine trees covering the area.

"I appreciate that Tiny, but if you don't know where you're going, how the hell you gonna know when you get there?'' Spahr quipped back.

''Let's get serious for a second.'' Spahr began to move around in front of the men once again.

''When Major Dixon first came out here, he had a gentleman named Quong with him. In case some of you couldn't guess, Quong is Vietnamese and recently escaped from Vietnam. He brought with him what the intelligence community believes to be irrefutable proof of American POWs still in country. We're going to go get them and bring them home!''

A simultaneous outburst came from the men at this statement.

''Let's go tonight.''

''All right!''

''Damn! Drake, trade with me! Let me go in your place!''

''Your ass, Reynolds. I hope you barf your guts while you circle when I'm on the ground.''

''We've been operating on generalities since we started this one. Tonight I'll give the team leaders an in-depth briefing and tomorrow's practice raid will be as realistic as we can make it. If you have questions, hold them until after tomorrow morning. I think most of them will be answered then. One more thing. Is there anyone who needs to update their emergency data packet? Scottie, I know you got married since last time. Is your stuff up to speed?'' Although Spahr was mission oriented, he still had a compassion for his men.

''Roger, sir. I'm straight. My insurance, will and everything is okay.'' Sergeant Winfield Scott, the only black and medic on the primary team, was one of the most respected members.

''Hell, Scottie, what do you need a will for? What are you going to leave her? Some no sweat pills and a half dozen unused body bags?''

"Screw you, Tiny! At least they won't have to cut me in half to get me in a bag. Say, if you buy the farm, where do you want to be planted, in Texas and Oklahoma or Texas and Arkansas?"

Sergeant Tiny Holt stood six feet seven inches tall and weighed over two hundred fifty pounds. He had needed a waiver for both his height and weight in order to join the Army.

"I'd like to see the officers in my tent for a few minutes. I think the rest of you should just cool it until we eat. Thank you and good luck."

Once inside the tent serving as his headquarters, Spahr brought his team leaders up to date.

"Gentlemen, we leave in seven days. We will be on the ground in eight and back home in nine." He stopped to open a large white plastic cooler and take out a six pack of chilled beer. Without asking, he handed one to each of the men. "I don't want to sound like the grim reaper but this one is gonna be a real bitch. Morgan, you were with me in Central America when we went in last year. Well, compared to this one, that was a piece of cake."

The men waited quietly for him to finish. "I'll have maps and satellite photos prior to departure. With them and the mock-up we've been using, we should be in pretty good shape. Our biggest asset is Quong."

"Yes sir. He gave us a hell of an advantage with his details. When we get back, I hope we get a chance to thank him." As Captain Miller spoke, he opened another beer and pulled a second six pack from the cooler. He slid the beer across the top of the wooden field desk around which they sat.

"If this hummer goes like it should, you won't have to wait, Jake. Quong will open the door on your plane when it hits the ground."

"You mean he's going with us, Colonel?"

"Not quite; I mean he's already on the ground. He's back in Vietnam!"

Miller almost dropped his beer. "Fuck me to tears! You mean he escaped and now he's gone back. The guy's nuts! He could be Special Forces already."

"Yeah, he sounds like he's already snake-eater qualified," Morgan added.

"On the surface it does sound like he's got more balls than brains, but I suspect it goes deeper than that." Spahr turned to Dixon. "Tom, maybe you can tell us some of the whys about Quong."

"Sir, I'm not sure even he knows why he agreed to do it. He's very close to a sister who's still in country. I suspect that she may find her way to the pick-up point with him." This was the first time Dixon had mentioned this possibility.

"I don't like having a last minute addition, Major. Perhaps you should have told us about this earlier." Spahr sounded more stern than Dixon had ever heard. "Do you have any other surprises for us?"

"No surprises, Colonel. Until this morning, I hadn't even thought about his sister. If she's anything like him, you won't have to worry about her. And, I suspect, Colonel, if you or anyone on the ground decide not to bring her back if Quong has her with him, none of us may make it."

"Dixon . . . you and I will talk about this later." Spahr left the tent.

For the next five days, training was intensified with emphasis on an early morning raid and another one just after darkness settled in over the Carolina pines. The fifth day was spent on a concentrated effort on the firing and demo ranges.

The main assault team carried Soviet built AK-47's. This was done not because it is a better weapon than the

American M-16, but rather because it was felt that if any shooting started once the team was on the ground the familiar sounds might be mistaken for drunk Vietnamese firing off a few rounds. This momentary confusion could possibly give the team the advantage they needed.

In addition, each man carried a 9mm pistol equipped with a silencer. Every other man carried a protective mask and three canisters of CS or CN gas. If necessary, they would drop to the back of the raiding party to cover their withdrawal with gas. Each man carried three grenades, two concussion or stunners and one fragmentation. Almost every man's harness had a vicious looking knife strapped upside down on the left strap. Inside the heel plate of one boot was the man's dog tag. Prior to leaving, they would be given an escape map printed on waterproof silk, a small roll of piasters and a small blister pack containing five white tablets and a red capsule.

The white tablets were Benzedrine, "hill climbers." They were to be used if the men needed a burst of speed. If they found themselves in an escape and evasion position, they could take the hill climbers and run all the way to Bangkok. No one asked about the red capsule. No one had to.

Plastic explosives were preformed and prepared in satchel charges. Small canvas stretchers with telescoping aluminum poles, similar to those on a camera tripod, were given to the men without protective masks. With this distribution of arms and equipment, each man carried approximately the same weight. The two largest pieces, a pair of twenty-four inch carbon steel bolt cutters and a small portable aceteline gas cutting torch, were scheduled to be used if necessary, then discarded. Each piece of equipment had been carefully stripped of all identification numbers, marks or makers' names.

* * *

If tne men on the ground at the Air Force base did not know the large plane was about to land, they would have no warning of its approach or existence. It circled once, then came in as silently as a cloud drifting aimlessly across the moonless night.

On the ground the men were beginning to feel the first hits as their bodies pumped supercharges of adrenalin into them. The ones who had stood on a tarmac before on nights such as this had the advantage of experience. The virgins on the team stood in silent anticipation.

As the first plane rolled to a stop, the team leader, Captain Miller, called off the name of each man as he stood in line and prepared to move to the waiting plane. "Lee, Nelson, Holt, Scott." By the time he finished his team, he turned to the last man standing on the runway. "Okay, Major, you got reservations for this circle jerk? I can give you a window seat if you're a big tipper, otherwise you can ride in the cattle car with the rest of the animals."

Dixon decided to let the comments pass. He could not determine if they were in jest or sarcastic. Either way, he would know the team's feeling toward him in a little over twenty-two hours.

"By the way, Captain, I hope you're not superstitious. You're the thirteenth man to load tonight." With that Dixon entered and took a seat along the wall of the plane.

The first leg of the flight took them across the northern edge of the United States, then out over the Pacific to Alaska. The decision not to fly over Canada for security reasons cost the team time in the air; however, the mission or the aircraft could not be explained if a crash or emergency landing was necessary, even in a friendly nation.

The refueling in Alaska marked the last time either of the two planes were scheduled to touch ground until they reached Vietnam.

Colonel Spahr had flown ahead of the two ships and was waiting in Alaska. Although he planned to give a small pep talk to the teams, his main purpose was to give the two crews their flight plan and in-air refueling points. Up until that time, the crew knew only that they had volunteered to fly a live mission, destination unknown.

A hot meal was brought out to the planes and three boxed flight meals per man was placed on board each ship. The men ate in silence as the refueling was completed.

"Hey, Doc. You got anything for a bad case of the shits? After eating MRE's back at Bragg for the last month, my tender young body may not know how to handle real food." Staff Sergeant Tiny Holt was the first to finish eating.

"How about a cork?" Doc replied.

"You don't need to worry about the shits. You better be thinking about lead poisoning," Sergeant Tomczah chided.

"Would someone please inform our token peasant of eastern European ancestry that my physician has specifically prohibited me from taking lead internally. He reports that nine out of ten top Fayetteville doctors have concluded that the practice can be extremely hazardous to one's health." Tiny spoke in a proper dialogue in his imitation of an English gentleman.

"Did he just say something about me being a Pollock."

"Ow, my aching ass. Here we go with the Pollock jokes again." Someone spoke from across the plane.

For over an hour the men traded jokes and war stories. Very few of the stories were new as these sessions occurred many times during training, especially on flights prior to jumps.

"You O.K., doc?" Lt. Nelson spoke to the team medic, Staff Sergeant Scott. "You don't look so good." He stood and crossed the aisle to take a seat next to the medic.

"No sweat, sir. I've just been thinking."

"This is not a good time to be doing a lot of deep thinking. You want to talk about it?"

"Don't get the wrong idea. I've been thinking about this plane we're on. You know, I've flown on and jumped out of everything the Army and the Air Force has. I even made a HALO from a B-52 one night in Nevada. On every one of those I could hear the noise of the plane. It sounded like a plane. Like we were flying." He leaned close to the Lieutenant as if to whisper.

"Do you realize we're talking in a normal voice. You ever rode in a military plane where you didn't have to yell to be heard? Colonel Spahr called this the Black Watch. I hope it's not the black death . . . especially for this black man."

Nelson knew the conversation was over. Scott turned in the seat and silently faced forward.

The two planes were met by tankers about 800 miles north of the Phillipines where they went through an in-air refueling. This would give both planes sufficient fuel to hit the target and leave Vietnam's air space prior to requiring another fueling.

The men broke up the flight by reading and playing cards. If it had been possible for an uninformed individual to observe the men, they would have appeared like almost any other group of trans-Pacific passengers, the main exception being that these passengers were armed to the teeth with an exotic array of weapons; and there was a distinct possibility that some of them were making a one-way flight.

The aircraft commander, an Air Force Lieutenant Colonel, called Captain Miller to the flight deck.

"Captain, we're about ten minutes from hitting Vietnamese airspace. I think you better get your men ready. We're less than an hour from touchdown. You got your strobe light and signal transmitter?"

"Roger, I've got one, my XO has a set and my security team has one." Miller patted the high intensity signal light he would use as a last minute signal for pick-up if the signal transmitter was lost or damaged.

The plan called for each of the transmitters to be activated when the man carrying it crossed the rice paddy on the return to the airfield. A triple signal was not necessary for pick-up. One activation would bring the plane in. By the time the transmitters were activated there would be little need for radio silence, so the teams could coordinate with each other and the ship if necessary.

Miller came back and called Lt. Nelson and Dixon over to where he stood. "Major, we're about thirty minutes from touchdown. Colonel Spahr gave me this to give to you. He said it was from Burkhalter. I got it in Alaska." He slowly handed the small folded envelope to Dixon.

"Look, I don't know what's in it, or why he wanted me to wait until now. We're not going to have a hell of a lot of time to discuss it. It's just about time to unass the A.O."

As Dixon opened the envelope, Miller turned to Nelson. "Get the men up. Do a final equipment check then get them in order by the door. Set 'em up like a jump stick. Sergeant Lee, Harry? You're in charge when the door opens. Get these thugs out and on the ground. Don't get too anxious when you get out. Don't forget we've got one friendly on the ground out there somewhere. He's going to give you two flashes with a red light. We respond with one, then get two more from him. Don't forget two, one, two, just like at Bragg."

Miller turned back to Dixon who was tearing the note into small pieces.

"Everything O.K., Major?"

"Yeah, it was just a little love note from the boss."

He barely got the words out when the plane cut power and touched the runway.

A team of American combat personnel was on the ground in Vietnam for the first time since the American Marines left the U.S. Embassy on the last chopper out of Saigon on 30 April 1975.

CHAPTER 13

The warm, moist Vietnamese night air lay heavy, as the men rushed silently from the slowly rolling aircraft. All loose gear had been neatly taped with black rubber bindings, making the men as soundproof as possible. The only sound from the airfield was the metallic grating of the perforated steel planking runway as the plane rolled across it. By the time the last man jumped effortlessly the three feet from the open tail ramp to the ground, the plane was beginning to make its pivot, thus allowing the blackness of the Vietnamese sky to reclaim and shelter the team's only link to the outside world.

Dixon and Miller moved silently across the width of the runway from the south side of the hardstand to the north.

"Miller, over here," Harry Lee was quietly calling the two men. Once on the ground, each man was referred to only by last name. On teams working together as a unit for months on end, each man usually picked up a distinct code or nickname. With this team being drawn from the larger detachment at Bragg, this was not feasible. In either case, no one used a rank designation when talking. To do so meant not only identifying the ranking members of the team, but it also ensured a fine of at least a beer party for the team and a probable fight between the parties involved.

"I've got a response to my signal. I think I've located Quong. I'm going to go through the signal one more time. Nelson move down his way. If the guy out there with the light fucks it up, it'll be the last button some zip ever pushes."

The two, one, two, signal was repeated flawlessly.

"Stand by, Dixon," Miller whispered. "Nelson should bring him back to us and we can get the hell off this airstrip."

The plane had returned, as silently as it arrived, to the Vietnam night. There were now thirteen Americans awaiting a signal to move, to begin an operation to free at least one of their comrades. If their planning and practice raids were accurate, they would be back in less than thirty-five minutes, ready for pick-up. If anything had been miscalculated or went wrong, it would be the longest thirty minutes they would ever spend.

Two men made their way to the location where Miller and Dixon waited. In the darkness Nelson was easily discernible because of his physical size and the outline of the equipment he wore. The second figure was smaller and wore only a shirt, pants and shoes. It was Quong.

"I got him, Miller. It's our old friend. Says he's been waiting out here for two days." Nelson spoke in a quick whisper. As he spoke, Quong stared hard at the figure crouched next to Miller. He did not dare believe his eyes. Dixon was the first to speak as the two men drew closer.

"Quong, ahn toi. We will talk later." As he spoke, Dixon grasped the man whom he had just called "brother" quickly by the shoulder.

"Yes, my brother, I have much to say, but tonight I worry for your life. Beth will think . . ."

"You guys can renew old acquaintances later. Right

now, we've got a mission. Quong, you're up. Phillips is on point, you're with him. Dixon, if you'd care to join us, we'll be leaving." An almost sinister smile came to Miller's face when he threw his last barb at Dixon.

Dixon made a feeble attempt to soften the atomsphere as the men started to move out.

"If this is the way you treat your guests, remind me never to accept your invitation to a party."

Miller whirled and almost spat back at him. "You're not my guest. I didn't invite you here. As far as I'm concerned, you're like a kid brother I've got to babysit. It's going to be a pain in the ass, but I've got to do it."

"Great. Now we both know the rules. You worry about the mission. I can take care of me." Dixon almost moved out of range of even his loud whisper as he slid past Miller to stay with the team.

Sergeant Lee stopped beside Miller. "Come on guys, we don't need that out here. You two can have a nutcutting back at Bragg. We're gonna need all the help we can get out here tonight."

The two thousand meters were covered in less than the time they had allocated, thus giving them almost two extra minutes in their schedule.

The point element stopped as soon as they could clearly see the back wall around the compound. Quong pointed to where one guard was asleep in an old wooden chair, his rifle laying across his lap. The guard had no idea how deep his sleep was about to become.

Once the remainder of the team pulled up to the last bit of cover prior to approaching the wall, Miller gave the signal to move on the sleeping guard.

To kill an armed enemy is an impersonal act. Very few times do the two combatants ever even see each other. This was different. Miller gave a signal which activated a man who, without thinking or rationalization, was to slip some fifty meters to a sleeping guard and then, quickly and silently, slit his throat.

The order was executed flawlessly. After dragging the lifeless body to a paddy dike and placing it on the far side, the point element signaled the rest of the men to advance. When Sergeant Lee came by, he picked up the dead guard's rifle and gave it to Quong.

Quong had been born and lived all his life in a country at war. For the first time in his life he had been placed in a position where he was expected to take an active, aggressive role in that war.

Less than twenty feet from the point where the men were now crossing the wall was a long, low building. Days of extensive and intensive training had made them intimately familiar with its purpose and its contents. Eddie Wilson was inside.

* * *

Throughout his years as a prisoner, Eddie had gone through many emotional and psychological phases. He had periods where he tried to do as much simple physical exercise as his food ration would allow. He went through a mental exercise phase where he pictured himself a great thinker and philosopher. His most devastating times were his agnostic and incredulous periods.

During those times, he gave up on his ability to believe in himself or anyone or anything else. He often sat, for hours, on the floor in the corner of his cell. Deep within the far recesses of his brain a small signal was sent throughout his body. It was if the signal said, "Let's pull ourselves together and get Eddie out of this corner. If we don't we're going to die here." Fortunately, the signal was well received and each of the periods lasted only about two weeks.

Eddie was now in a sleepless period, waking up at all hours of the night. He felt, when morning came, that he had slept less than two hours all night.

Many times as he lay in the limited security of his mosquito net covered rack, he reflected over his past. When he felt gutsy he even speculated on his future.

Barring some unforseen illness or disease, he could last as a prisoner of war for years. He got enough food to keep him at his present weight of about one hundred twenty pounds. This was down from the one-seventy-five he'd been when he was captured. At five feet eleven inches, he could stand the lighter weight better than some of his taller friends.

"Friends," he said aloud. "I haven't seen some of those people in over fifteen years and I still call them friends. Hell, I haven't even seen my family since the last week I was home before coming to Vietnam. I wonder how many of them are still alive. I'm sure Dad's gone now. Maybe Mom, too. Neither of them was in the best of health when I left. God knows what happened to them when they heard about me."

Eddie shifted in his rack, trying to get as comfortable as possible without disturbing the carefully secured mosquito net covering him.

His solitude was momentarily broken by the sound of the guard outside his cell being changed. Eddie raised up to a sitting position and recognized Minh, the Vietnamese he called Jack, outside his door.

As was his custom, Minh shined an old Army flashlight in the room. As usual, when Eddie was awake and the light flashed across his rack, he openly flipped his guard the finger.

"Sleep Wil Son. Son Bitch! Ngay mai anh noi duyen voi dai tai."

Jack mixed English and Vietnamese as he tried to talk

occasionally with Wilson.

"Right, Jack. I'll check my social calendar. I'll probably have time to see your colonel tomorrow," said Wilson in response to the guard's announcement that he was to see the commandant tomorrow.

As the two of them bantered, Eddie saw two shadows move across the open end of the building. At first glance he thought nothing unusual; however, when two more shadowy forms slipped into position by the first two, Eddie strained to see and hear from inside his rack.

"Easy boy, you've been here too long to get spooked by things that go bump in the night."

"Sleep Wil Son! Go now."

There was definite reaction outside when Eddie's name was used.

"Please God, if I'm going crazy or dying and those are angels outside looking for me, let it be quick," he mutterd half aloud.

Eddie pulled back the mosquito net and slid out of his self-imposed nightly exile from the world.

"Jack, la day, come here. Let's talk." He walked over to the bars. "Look this way. Let's give you an English lesson."

Eddie was facing the open area between the building and the kitchen when, over Jack's left shoulder, he saw a sight he had prayed for, waited for, almost given up on in the last eight years. A round-eyed American soldier was crouched with a knife in his right hand, less than six feet from the door to his cell.

Like a dying man making a deathbed confession, Eddie spoke quickly and on impulse. "Jack, you're the only friend I've got here. I'd hate to see you hurt."

Staff Sergeant Larry Drake heard Wilson and in midair changed direction with his heavy handed stroke so the guard felt the butt of the knife across the back of his head rather than the blade across his throat. The guard crumpled and fell into Drake's waiting arms.

Outside, Lt. Nelson placed his men near the wall. They could now cover the two buildings the raiders were scheduled to enter.

Quong, Dixon and Miller were in the building before Jack hit the ground. Quong immediately recognized the prone figure.

"He is now dead? Yes!" Quong spoke to Drake.

"No, your man saved his life. He'll be out for a while, though. He won't give us any static."

"Will somebody please tell me what's going on. If this is a dream I'm gonna be some kind of pissed when I wake up." Wilson stood with his hands on the bars to his cell door.

"It's no dream. You're going home. Compliments of the US Army Special Forces. Drake, cut this lock; we're wasting time." Miller quietly, coolly gave the order to free Wilson.

"Do you know where there are any others? We think there are more Americans here, and we don't have much time to find them," Miller spoke as the bolt cutters bit into the heavy brass lock separating the two men.

The lock was removed and the door to freedom swung open. For the first time in eight years, Wilson stood with freedom only one step away. He remained motionless, unable to take the step.

"Come on, man. Let's get the fuck out of here." Miller took him by the arm.

"It's okay. Trust me. We're going to get you out of here. It's really over." Dixon moved past Miller and into the cell with Wilson. "There are enough of us outside to do it. We can make it." It was as if he was talking to a vicious animal. "Put your trust in us. We'll get you out."

"Wait. Wait a minute," Wilson hesitated a second then walked over to his large wooden box. He opened it and removed a ball of string the size of a baseball and a wooden pencil about four inches long. "Okay. Now we can go."

As he took his first step toward freedom, he clutched the string and the pencil in his two hands joined together in front of his chest, much like a child would do with his teddy bear.

"There are two more cells in here. They have two old Regional Force commanders in them. Could you cut their locks and give them a chance to go home, too?"

As Drake moved down the corridor, Quong looked at the prone figure of the man who had been living with Bea.

"It is not good to leave him like this. If he wakes, he will warn others. He should die, I think."

A statement like this was totally out of character for Quong. Dixon wondered if he had changed in other ways since his return.

Drake returned with two almost emaciated Vietnamese.

"I doubt they can make it home, but tell them to wait here and keep quiet. They can have the guard's weapon." Miller turned from Quong back to Wilson. "Now, are there other Americans here?"

"I've seen at least two. As near as I can tell, they're in the long building across the compound. They're probably in the near end." As he spoke, Wilson pointed between the buildings. "The big one in the middle is the kitchen. It's clear at night. There should only be one guard, just like here. There's a wall beyond the building. I'm afraid I can't help much more than that. I've never been there."

"We'll be back to get you after we spring them. Drake, give me the cutters. You stay with these guys. Put some luminous tape on them, so we can identify them in the dark, just in case the shooting starts." As he spoke, Miller avoided even looking at Dixon.

The men moved single file in the shadows from Wilson's cell to the kitchen, then around it to a covered point approximately twenty meters from the second building which Wilson said contained Americans.

"Okay guys, this is where it might get hairy. Be alert. Let's go." Miller, still crouched, moved up with Phillips and Quong on point.

The three men moved cautiously around the side to the open door on the front of the long cement block building. Quong peered cautiously inside where he saw two guards. From his vantage point he could see at least four cell doors.

"One guard here, one down there," Quong pointed as he reported to Miller. "I saw four doors but could not see inside them."

"Tiny, the one at the far end is yours. Phillips, you take the one inside the door. The rest of us will cover you." Miller looked at Dixon. "That is, unless you'd like to try to talk them out."

Before Dixon could respond, Sergeant Lee placed a firm hand on his arm. "Later; there'll be time for you two later," he said.

Once Tiny was in place, he gave a wave of his hand and he and Phillips entered the building. Unlike a few minutes earlier, there was no one around to plead for the guards' lives. In less than five seconds both were dead on the floor.

The sounds in the hallway woke the man sleeping in the first cell. Unlike the building where they found Eddie Wilson, these looked more like very low-rent apartments in the South Bronx than like cells for prisoners of war.

The man inside the first cell was sleeping on an old grey

steel army bunk with a dingy mattress covering the now sagging springs. Thin metal rods formed a frame over the bunk onto which a mosquito net had been carefully and neatly stretched. A low, wooden, three drawer cabinet stood in the near corner. A straight back chair was next to the bunk. Laying across the back of the chair was a pair of cutoff pants belonging to the man now awake under the net.

The door opened and he stepped halfway outside into the hallway. As he walked, he spoke sleepily to the now dead guard in a form of Vietnamese obtainable only after years of speaking the language on a daily basis.

Only Quong understood all the conversation, but even Dixon picked up enough to know the sleepy man was raising hell with the guard for disturbing him.

As Miller, Phillips and Holt opened the other three doors, Dixon entered the first cell. He quickly pushed the emerging resident back into the far corner. As he did so, he placed his silenced 9mm pistol under the man's chin.

"You've got five seconds to convince me not to kill you. Talk fast . . . one . . ."

"Wait! Wait! Who are you?" The man stood braced in a corner, his eyes wide with fear and disbelief at what he was seeing.

"Two! Quong, tell Miller and the others these bastards are not POWs. Be cautious! Three!"

"Okay, okay. I'm an American. I am a prisoner, but, I'm like a trustee, you know. Can't you put that gun down?" The man was about Dixon's age but his overall excellent physical condition was evidence of more than trustee status.

By now three men had been taken from their rooms and were herded into the room with Dixon.

As the three men were half pushed into the room, one immediately caught Dixon's eye. He was a tall, thin man. He stood over six feet and, even under these conditions, he appeared to be in near excellent physical shape. His most distinguishing characteristic, though, was a crop of shoulder length bright red hair.

"Whoever or whatever these guys are, they're coming with us. Now!" Miller faced the four men. "Do you come on your own or do we take you by force? It makes no difference to me."

As he spoke, the red-haired man standing nearest Quong moved like a mongoose attacking a cobra. He grabbed the assault rifle from Quong and pointed it at Miller. "Not me man. I'm not going anywhere. You're not taking me back for a firing squad just so some . . ."

Before he could finish, an explosion ripped through the upper right portion of his chest as Dixon fired one silenced round at the man who had quickly slipped his rifle from safe to fire and was preparing to kill Miller.

For a second Miller started to speak. Before he could say anything Dixon looked him in the eye and said, "That's one you owe your little brother."

"Doc, check this guy out, then hit these others. Tiny, if he needs help, hold these guys. If they give us any static, shoot them." Miller watched the medic as he first checked the wounded man on the floor then prepared three syringes with a mixture which would knock the men out in less than thirty seconds.

"Make sure you don't give too much to Big Red," said Dixon as he continued to hold his pistol on the men. "He and I and the boss have a few things to talk over when we get back."

"Harry, start putting some demo charges under the building and along the wall. Give us a three minute fuse. And put some artillery simulators out there, too. Maybe the sound will throw them off. Doc, get us four stretchers ready. We're gonna have to pull security in here to help us carry them." Miller was now in complete control as he directed the men.

The signal was passed to Nelson and half the security team joined the men in the building.

The now sleeping men were placed on the stretchers, and Harry was told to pull the fuses.

Before they lifted the stretchers, Quong spoke to the two Americans.

"Dixon, Miller, there is one more place we must go. It is on our way out. We must get one more person from the kitchen." Quong was not asking. His tone of voice left no doubt the stop would be made.

Harry came back inside. "It's three minutes and counting. Let's unass the A.O."

Miller looked first at Quong then Dixon. "We've got one more stop, guys. It's on the way out. I think this one's for Quong."

The men waited outside the kitchen in the shadows as Quong entered and called softly in the darkness, "Bea! Bea oi! La day! We must hurry."

Slowly the woman emerged from under a counter in the cooking area. "Is it real, Quong? Are we really leaving? Have they come for us like they promised?" She moved across the room and placed her arms around him. For the first time in his adult life, Quong saw his sister cry. "It's really true? They're not going to leave us like in Saigon?"

"No, em. This time you will go all the way to America. But now, we must hurry."

When the two of them emerged from the old kitchen and Dixon saw her for the first time, it was if he, too, was helping a member of his own family escape. Until that moment he didn't realize how much he had become personally involved with Quong and his sister.

Quong placed Bea's hand in Dixon's. "Bea, our brother Dixon will take you to America. Do not release his hand.

No matter what happens, he will get you there."

"Miller, we've got less than two minutes to get out of this compound before the north end is blown to shit." Harry was looking anxiously at his watch.

The stretcher bearers moved onto the wall as Miller, Lee, Dixon and Quong stopped for Eddie Wilson and the still unconscious guard. "We'll take turns carrying his ass. We're out of stretchers."

"I wasn't crazy! You're the broad with the camera! You really did say smile, didn't you?" Wilson was beside himself with excitement as he recognized Bea and began to put some of the pieces together.

"Let's go. We can work out the details later." Miller led the way. The last man had cleared the wall when the first charge exploded. Almost instantaneously the high-pitched shrill whistle of an artillery round was produced by a simulator. Two other explosions could be heard in rapid succession.

Sergeants Lee and Holt were carrying the stretcher with the one Dixon called Big Red on it.

"That should keep them busy for a while. That's like one time I set some charges, me and Tomczak, up around Zion . . ."

"Aw, shit, Harry. Hold the war stories at least until we get these guys off our ass."

"You'll be sorry, you big son-of-a-bitch. What if I get killed and you don't find out how it ends."

"They all end the same way. You blow up every fucking thing in sight. Like back there. I saw you set a charge under the end of the kitchen. I can't believe you're gonna blow up their mess hall."

The men were half running in single file across the rice paddies when the area to their rear began to light up as spotlights around the corners of the compound were activated.

"Holy shit! Who turns on a spotlight in the middle of a firefight." Sergeant Gary Richards was rear security and was almost running backwards watching the activity. "Ain't they never seen no war movies? Everybody knows you turn the lights out when the shooting starts." He almost yelled at the men ahead of him. "Ya'll better eat a couple of them hill climbers. This shit is about to get sticky!"

The dull, thud! thud! of rounds from a fifty caliber machine gun hitting the ground around them was the first indication that they had been spotted. That was quickly followed by small arms fire. At first it seemed sporadic, then more concentrated as the Vietnamese began to get their range.

The signal for the plane to land was given and a second signal indicating they were in contact was transmitted to the back-up plane.

Miller was looking back over his shoulder when he saw his first man go down. Richards was hit. "Dixon! Lee! Richards is hit. Dixon, give me a hand. The rest of you keep going."

As Dixon turned to help Miller, he looked at Bea whose hand he still held. "Stay with Quong. I'll be back in a minute." He released her hand; however, she continued to hold his.

"No. I will go with you. Please do not leave me." There was fear and sincerity in her voice.

With Bea in tow, Dixon helped Miller get the young sergeant on his feet. The round in his shoulder knocked him down and might have broken his shoulder blade, but he was still able to walk.

"Dump your harness. Get rid of your gear. Here, let me have your weapon." Miller helped the man up. He was half lifting, half dragging him as they began to move again.

The point team with Phillips and Quong had reached the edge of the runway at approximately the same spot where Quong met then less than one hour earlier.

As the men carrying stretchers made it to the runway, they placed their burdens on the ground, then returned to help the others and to start laying down covering fire for the men bringing up the rear. Even in the almost still dead night air, a few breezes stirred the gas thrown as they left the compound. It began to start making their eyes water.

Miller had Richards on his feet and the two of them were half running towards the runway. Dixon, with Bea still hoiding onto him like a small child, was less than one hundred yards from the runway when the first round tore into him. Before he even felt it, another round found its way into the body of the dainty woman holding his hand.

For the second time in his life, Dixon found himself lying face down, wounded, in the mud of a Vietnamese rice paddy. Unlike the last time, this one hurt. It was serious and he knew instinctively that he could, very soon, be near death.

As he lay in the mud, he felt as if everything was now running in slow motion around him. He knew Miller was less than ten feet away but it would take days, perhaps months, for him to reach the spot where he now lay.

A pressure on his right hand brought him back to reality. Bea must also still be alive. She was gently squeezing his hand calling Quong's name.

Softly, she cried as she lay, blood covered, next to Dixon.

"Quong, Dix On, please take me. Do not leave me." Even as her voice began to grow faint from a loss of blood, she continued to plead for the one thing that had meant so much to them in the last few months. "Please take me. Quong take . . ."

"Doc! Get two stretchers over here. Dixon and the woman's been hit."

As soon as Quong heard Miller, he left the runway and ran to their side.

"They are not dead? They cannot die because of me. If they die, then I will return to the compound. Every man there will also die!"

"Help us get them on a stretcher. Quong, you help carry the woman." Miller kneeled beside Dixon.

"The woman, as you call her, is my sister! She is the one who gave the information which brought you here!" As he spoke, Quong was unconsciously fingering the trigger on the rifle of Dixon's he had picked up.

"They're still alive, Quong. They've been hit bad but they're still with us. Now help get them on the plane while we all still have a chance."

Everyone there, including Quong, crouched at the edge of the runway and lay down a wicked wall of fire as the large black plane rolled to a near stop behind them. The men virtually threw the Americans on the stretchers from the second building on board.

As they were loading Dixon and Bea, Wilson reached out to help with the stretcher on which Bea now lay near death. "I owe this little lady a lot. If it wasn't for her I wouldn't be here." For the first time in years, Wilson was around and talking to people who were not his captors and guards.

As Bea was transferred to a cot which folded down over the seats, Wilson gently pulled her long black hair from across her face. As he did so, he couldn't help but notice what a beautiful woman she was. As the medic, Doc Scott, inserted an I.V. tube to feed blood clotter into her,

Wilson leaned over the woman. He gently kissed her cheek and whispered, in a voice that only the two of them would ever hear or understand, a single word. SMILE!

CHAPTER 14

The plane turned rapidly at the west end of the long strip and quickly began its trip down the runway, gaining speed for lift-off and safety. Unfortunately, between the two was a small army of very irate Vietnamese, the majority of whom were now firing indiscriminately at the aircraft. Most of them were using a variety of small arms, and the few hits the ship took did relatively little damage.

A simultaneous cheer went up as the men felt the plane break loose and lift off from Vietnam.

"Captain Miller, Major Dixon, can you two come up? There's a radio call for you up front." The crew chief called for them over the internal public address system.

"What do I tell them, Doc? Is he going to make it?" Miller stopped and talked to his medic who, along with Tiny Holt, was working furiously with the added medical supplies now available to them on the aircraft.

"He's tough and he deserves to make it. Both of them do, but they need more than a canker mechanic. I think he took it in the spine. We may have done more damage hauling him around. The girl, jeez, I don't know. She's loosing blood faster than I can get it back in her. They need a real hospital, real doctors. Richards will be all right, but you gotta help these two." Doc continued to work as rapidly as he could.

Quong and Wilson were now kneeling beside the two cots, both asking if there was any help they could give.

Miller made the walk to the front of the aircraft. As soon as he got to the flight deck, the crew all flashed him a thumbs up and offered congratulations to him and his team.

"I've got a man on here who wants to talk to you." The pilot handed a headset and microphone to Miller. "It's a secure frequency. I've cut it in for only you. No one else here will monitor."

"This is Oxfly Mike, over." Miller used his prearranged call sign for the first time on this operation.

"Oxfly Mike, this Oxfly Bravo. What is your current status? You can give it in the clear; this line is secure."

"We got Wilson. He's in good shape all around. We also got four others. I'm not sure yet who or what they are. We also picked up a Vietnamese guard. He was with Wilson and seemed like some kind of friend or something so we took him as security. One of my men, Sergeant Richards, is also hit but not too bad." Miller stopped in order to let the information sink in and gather his thoughts prior to telling Colonel Spahr about Dixon and Bea.

"Colonel, we've got two people that we've got to get to the closest hospital. They won't make it back to the States. It's Major Dixon and Quong's sister. They were helping me with Richards when they got it. What's the closest place we can land with a hospital?"

"Your pilot has an emergency landing clearance that will get you to a hospital in a little over an hour. General Burkhalter will get on the line with you and him right now. You'll make it, Jake, all of you. Here's the General. He wants to talk to you."

"Tell me about these others you got. Do you know anything about them yet? Are they all American?"

Burkhalter asked anxiously.

"Roger, sir, they all seem to be Americans. One of them was babbling about going back to a firing squad. He was about to shoot me when Dixon greased him. He was hit bad but he'll make it. Your man Dixon is a dead eye with a Browning. He . . ."

"Tell me what they look like. Give me a physical description of the men, Miller."

"Four white males. All about five-ten to six-one tall. One of them's got a head full of bright red hair. He and Dixon . . ."

"Tell me about him. The guy with red hair, tell me about him." Burkhalter almost sounded greedy for information.

"All I know is what I told you, sir. We had to have Doc give them a mickey to get them to come along quietly. Dixon said one thing, though; he told me to take good care of Big Red. He said the three of you had a lot to talk about."

"Captain, you've got to make Dixon understand something. If he's dying I owe it to him. Tell him the boss said it looks like he got Big Red. Mention the note you gave to him prior to the operation. You did give it to him, didn't you? He'll understand. He's got to know that. Do you read me?" Burkhalter was emphatic in his tone.

"Sir, I'll do my best but you better let me get back to him. I don't think we've got a lot of time to screw around with."

"I understand, Captain. Thanks to all of you. Now let me speak to the pilot. We'll get you to a hospital." After that, the line went silent as the General signed off.

Miller made his way back to Dixon. "Can he hear me, Doc? Have you been able to talk to him?"

"He's hardly responding to anything. I've got the bleeding slowed down some but I'm out of O positive blood for him. That's my last unit hanging now. When that one's gone, we're gonna be in deep shit."

"Maybe not. I'm O positive. You can do a live bleed with me. But first I've got to make him understand something." Miller leaned close to the man's ear.

"Big Red, Dixon, Big Red! You got Big Red." Midway through his second repetition of this, Dixon's eyes fluttered lightly.

"Keep him talking. Keep him conscious. That'll help keep him out of shock." Doc spoke to Miller.

Dixon laboriously responded to Miller.

"Red . . . a traitor. U Minh. Killed boss's son . . ." Even these few words from Dixon were taking their toll.

"Quong, you and Wilson stay with him. I'm going to go wake Red up. How long before that stuff wears off, Doc?"

"Any time now."

"I'm sorry this is not a first class return for you, Wilson. Maybe we can make it up to you when we get on the ground. You spent all those years in a POW camp, and then we make you work on the flight home." Miller patted the man on the shoulder as he stood up.

"Lieutenant Nelson. Let's see if we can't wake up Red Riding Hood and find out more about him. Take some cargo straps and lash all of them to their cots. I'm afraid if they move wrong I'd have to snuff 'em. For my little brother," he added.

Miller began to slap the drugged man firmly on the sides of his face. "Wake up you son-of-a-bitch! You're not hurt half as bad as you're gonna be if you don't wake up!" Again he slapped the red haired man who was now stirring and blinking his eyes as he slowly came into consciousness.

"Wait a minute! Wait. What the hell's going on? Who are you guys?"

"You don't ask questions. You just answer till I tell you otherwise." Miller leaned down and spoke almost nose-to-nose. "Who are you and why were you still in Vietnam? And what's your concern with a firing squad?"

"Maybe I know who he is." Eddie Wilson was standing over the cot containing the restrained man.

"Don't listen to that guy. He's been here so long he's liable to say anything. I'm an American. A prisoner. Just like him. Like the rest of them back there."

Wilson surprised even himself with his lack of hostility as he spoke to the two men. "Back in the U Minh, we heard about an American who had gone over to the side of the V.C. I don't know anyone, personally, who saw him, but everyone said he was tall and had red hair. They called him Big Red. Seems to me this guy's tall, and he's sure as hell got red hair. My guess is that you've solved the mystery of Big Red, Dai Uy!"

While the men questioned the now fully conscious person they called Big Red, Quong spoke softly to Bea. He spoke in Vietnamese, telling her how proud he was that she had tried to help another human being. He explained how Buddha would wait for her; and, if this was the time for her to make the journey, she would have many ancestral guides to take her through the darkness to the light.

He also told her that she should try to keep her life in this world as long as possible. Though Buddha was a just and loving god, he was not impatient and would understand if she did not wish to depart at this time.

He talked to her for over ten minutes and only an occasional nod from the medic confirmed that Bea had not already departed to the land of their ancestors.

Miller and Wilson returned to Quong's side. Miller looked at the ragged thin frame of Eddie Wilson as the man gently stroked the temple and side of Bea's face much like a father would do a sleeping daughter.

"Wilson, do you know who those other guys are or what they were doing there?" Miller asked as he, too, kneeled at the head of the two cots.

"The whole time I was there I only saw two other Americans, or at least I think they were American. One was a black guy; the other was white. I only saw them once about a year ago. They were in a jeep that passed me one day. As for the rest of these guys, beats the hell out of me."

"Captain! We're losing the Major!" Doc yelled across excitedly to Miller. "I've got no blood pressure. If you want to help him, lay down. Tiny! Get us a siphon hose going. We're gonna run it straight into the Major."

While Holt and Miller frantically set up to do a live transfusion, Doc started mouth to mouth resuscitation. Dixon responded with a faint heartbeat.

"Fifteen minutes to touchdown. Everyone please secure. Will a team officer come forward?" The pilot made a most welcome announcement.

"Nelson, take over. See if you can get through to Burkhalter. If you can, tell him Dixon understood his message. Say he told me about . . . no, that's enough. Just say he understood and that I want a pair of surgeons waiting for Dixon and Bea when this mother hits the ground."

Their two cots were side by side on the plane. Bea's was closest to the walls of the aircraft. Dixon's was beside her on the aisle.

As Quong kneeled between the two of them at their heads, he saw his past and future as both lay dying. Only a miracle of timing and medical skill could save either.

Bea traditionally was his responsibility, but now he was unable to help her. She would live or die, and he had no control over either.

With all her planning, Bea had not even considered the cruel fact that she, the strong one of the family, would exit Vietnam on a stretcher. For Quong, the worst part of it was that she would probably die never knowing the idea she conceived worked—just as she envisioned it: Quong left, told his story to the Americans, they believed him and they returned to successfully rescue Eddie Wilson and four others.

"Quong, she's gonna make it." Wilson was talking to him now. "I've been through a lot in the last eight years but I made it because I had a goal, a purpose. I knew someday I would go home. I didn't know how or when, but I knew it would happen. She's going home, too. But she's going with you to wherever you go. She may spend some time in a hospital but she'll spend more time with you back in the States. Don't you worry about little Smiley here, she's got what it takes. Both of them do."

Quong felt the gentle thump as the wheels hit the runway. It's strange, he thought as they began to slow down. They are about to take Bea and Dixon off and I do not even know where we are.

"There's a radio call for Quong," the pilot announced over the loudspeaker.

"Go ahead, I'll stay with her," Wilson urged him to take the call.

Once up front, the crew chief showed him how to use the headset. When he activated it, he heard the familiar voice of General Burkhalter.

"Quong, first let me say, personally and professionally, I want to thank you for everything you've done. We're going to do the absolute best we can for your sister and Major Dixon. I know you're on the ground now, so say a prayer for our two friends and let the medical personnel there show you what a good job they can do. I'll see you the next time you land. Out here."

By the time he returned to Bea, the plane had rolled quietly to a stop. The large rear door was slowly being lowered.

Soon Bea and Dixon would be in a real hospital. That was the best he could ask for now.

As soon as the door was halfway down, several men jumped inside the aircraft and began to check vital signs and start additional fluids, which Quong did not fully understand, in their veins.

Both Bea and Dixon had at least one doctor and several attending helpers. This pleased Quong, as he watched them being lifted from the plane and placed into the waiting ambulance.

Quong followed the rapidly moving stretchers out of the plane to the ambulance. Bea was placed in first, on the left side, then Dixon on the right. While the attendants were hanging the bottles overhead, Quong reached in and gently took Bea's hand. He held it for a second, then as gently as with his sister, he took Dixon's hand and held the two of them in his. He prayed, first to his God, then to Dixon's. As he slowly released the hands, he was shocked to see that after he took his away the two did not fall free. Dixon was still clinging to Bea.

Through freely flowing tears, Quong watched the ambulance disappear into the night.

"Quong oi! la day. You don't want us to leave your ass, do you?" Wilson was standing in the back of the plane extending a hand to pull Quong back into the craft for the remainder of the last journey to freedom for the two final victims of the war.